TROLLED

TROLLED

Steven Sandor

James Lorimer & Company Ltd., Publishers
Toronto

James Lorimer & Company Ltd., Publishers acknowledges the support of the Ontario Arts Council. We acknowledge the support of the Canada Council for the Arts which last year invested $24.3 million in writing and publishing throughout Canada. We acknowledge the Government of Ontario through the Ontario Media Development Corporation's Ontario Book Initiative.

Canada

The Canada Council for the Arts | Le Conseil des Arts du Canada

Ontario Arts Council
Conseil des Arts de l'Ontario

Library and Archives Canada Cataloguing in Publication

Sandor, Steven, 1971-, author
Trolled / Steven Sandor.

(Sports stories)
Issued in print and electronic formats.
ISBN 978-1-4594-1142-5 (paperback).--ISBN 978-1-4594-1143-2 (epub)

I. Title. II. Series: Sports stories (Toronto, Ont.)

PS8637.A547T76 2016 jC813'.6 C2016-902601-9
C2016-902602-7

James Lorimer & Company Ltd., Publishers
117 Peter Street,
Suite 304
Toronto, ON, Canada
M5V 0M3
www.lorimer.ca

Canadian edition
(978-1-4594-1142-5)
distributed by:
Formac Lorimer Books
5502 Atlantic Street
Halifax, NS, Canada
B3H 1G4

American edition
(978-1-4594-1145-6)
distributed by:
Lerner Publishing Group
1251 Washington Ave N
Minneapolis, MN, USA
55401

Canadian edition printed and bound in Canada.
United States edition printed and bound in Canada.
Manufactured by Friesens Corporation in Altona, Manitoba, Canada in July 2016.
Job #225178

CONTENTS

PROLOGUE

One. Two. Three. Breathe.

Andy's right arm broke through the surface. He reached forward and rotated his wrist so his thumb would be pointing downward when it plunged back into the water. He repeated the motion with his left arm, trying to keep his form as symmetrical as possible. Each stroke had to be a mirror image of the other. On every fourth stroke, he lifted his head just out of the water so he could take a quick breath. He didn't exhale until his head was back in the water. He controlled the pace at which he exhaled, almost as if he were whispering into the water, a line of bubbles rising from his face.

Coach Ocampo had hammered home the lesson. *If you exhale too quickly, your lungs will feel like they are going to burst. Nice and steady. Big splashes slow you down.*

Andy peered through the lenses of his grey no-fog goggles and saw the wall coming closer. Before getting to the wall, he rolled in the water, somersaulting and twisting at the same time. Now his feet were planted against the wall he'd been facing. He pushed off and shot off in the other direction.

One. Two. Three. Breathe. One. Two. Three. Breathe.

Andy was close to the wall at the other end. He reached for it. His fingers hooked onto the edge and his head broke the surface of the water. He looked at Coach Ocampo, who was standing on the deck of the Earnscliffe Recreation Centre pool. The coach had a stopwatch in his hand.

"Not bad," the coach said. "Good pace this morning."

Andy nodded as he bobbed in the deep end of his lane. He looked across the pool. There were about a dozen swimmers spread out over eight lanes. The breaststrokers shovelled away the water in front of them, rose to the surface and then plummeted down again. The backstrokers' goggles aimed upward as their arms windmilled past their ears. One swimmer in the far lane was doing the butterfly stroke, majestically smashing his arms into the water as if he were a human helicopter.

"Now arms only Andy!" cried the coach.

Andy crossed his legs so they would be immobilized. That way, he felt like he was dragging an anchor behind him. He began to swim with only his arms to pull him along.

One lap.

Two laps.

Three laps.

Four laps.

1 COBRA

Shoulders burning, Andy climbed out of the pool and, while dripping wet, did thirty push-ups right on the deck.

Nearby, a brand-new member of the City of Brampton swim team bolted out of the pool and toward the men's change room. The boy's hands were over his face. His cheeks bulged.

Andy saw the streams of orange puke oozing through the boy's fingers.

"It's a killer workout, first-timer!" Andy called out. "Next time, don't drink any juice before swimming. Anything acidy is coming right back up!"

Coach Ocampo looked at his clipboard and then at the boy who had puked before he could make it to the washroom. "I'll hose that down in a second. You may as well go in, rinse off and then come back right out here . . . what's your name? Ferguson? Yeah, Ferguson. Come right back out here because you still owe me a few more laps! Everybody pukes on their first day, so don't think throwing up gets you off easy!"

Enalyn Marquez, Andy's teammate on the COBRA swim club, was in the next lane.

"Poor new guy doesn't know what hit him." She laughed.

"He'll learn. I puked my guts out on the first day," said Andy.

"Working on your times, Andy?" Enalyn raised an eyebrow.

"If I can swim like this at summer provincials, I'll qualify."

"At this rate, you're going to be the youngest Canadian on the Olympic team."

Andy shrugged. "Dare to dream, right? And, well, if you work on that rotation, you can swim the time you need, too. You could be the next Miriam Said."

"Miriam Said. I wish. Seriously, Andy, I don't know if I can do it. I need to shave a half-second from my times, Andy. A whole half-second!"

★★★

Coach Ocampo blew the whistle that hung from the chain around his neck. "Okay guys, practice done! Be in the showers in five minutes! That's when the aquafit club takes over!"

Andy watched the younger swimmers roll the lane ropes into tubes. The giant clock at the far end read

6:55 a.m. Just enough time. He leaned over, grabbed a blue flutterboard and tossed it into the water.

"What are you doing?" asked the new kid.

"You'll see," Andy said.

He reached up and grabbed the end of the rope that hung from the ceiling.

"Okay new guy, this is what we do at the end of practice, as soon as the lane markers are gone. What we use this rope for . . ."

"Surfing!" cried the rest of the team, picking up on Andy's cue.

"Right. The goal is to swing into the pool, come down feet first and land on the flutterboard just right. Ninety-nine times out of a hundred, you hit the board, it goes flying in the air and . . . splashdown! But if you hit it just right, carrying enough momentum, you'll land on it and surf across the pool."

"Or you might break the flutterboard and Coach Ocampo has to pay for a new one," cried the coach.

Andy held out the end of the rope to the new kid. "Okay, here you go, rookie."

The new kid stepped forward. He took five quick steps, leapt up onto the rope and swung into the pool. He splashed in well short of the board.

"Not enough momentum!" Andy yelled.

"Show him how it's done!" came a voice from the crowd of swimmers.

"Yeah Andy, do it!"

Andy smiled. "Okay ladies and gentlemen. I can't let the crowd down."

He turned and jogged to the far wall of the pool enclosure. Then he pushed off like a sprinter, his bare feet splashing on the wet deck. He got close to the edge and leapt high onto the rope, trying to maintain as much speed as he could into the swing.

Andy saw the flutterboard coming closer. He knew that he had to drop as if he was going to land just short of it. His momentum would carry him forward, and he'd hit the target.

He dropped off the rope, getting ready to plant the left foot ahead of the right foot. If he landed with both feet together, he'd just fall right back.

Andy felt the board under his feet. He was gliding on top of the water! He skipped across the waves being created in the pool. He heard the cheers from his teammates.

And he heard Coach Ocampo: "Good stuff, Tiger Shark! If only they made flutterboard surfing an actual sport! I can only hope you apply yourself to your laps like you do your fun and games!"

Andy swam to the edge of the pool and climbed out onto the deck. The new kid stood over him.

"Tiger Shark? Why did coach call you Tiger Shark?"

Andy grabbed a towel and draped it around his shoulders. "Everyone on the team calls me Tiger Shark."

"Why is that your nickname?"

"'Cause I'm the fastest guy in the pool, and when you race against me, I devour you."

"Oh, cool."

"Well, I've got a cool nickname for you," Andy said, trying hard to suppress a snicker.

"Yeah?"

"Yeah, I'm gonna call you Superpuke."

The new kid turned red. "You can't do that!"

"Yeah, I just sorta did," said Andy, as he spun around and made a beeline for the change room. "See you outside, Superpuke."

***

Andy logged on to Skype. Enalyn was already online, as were some of his other COBRA teammates.

TIGERSHARK: So, this new guy, what's his story?

EN_MARQUEZ: I watched him for a bit. He isn't that fast. But it's just his first practice . . .

TIGERSHARK: En? You like this guy or something :) ???

EN_MARQUEZ: No. Jerk! :-

SCOTT13: This guy's new. And we all know what happens to new guys. INITIATION!

JAMIE_THE_EEL: Yup. And didn't you all notice this new guy had a nice, full head of hair?

EN_MARQUEZ: You guys are going to do this again? Really?

TIGERSHARK: It's settled then, right?

JAMIE_THE_EEL: I can bring the stuff.

TIGERSHARK: I can present him with a new team swimming cap.

SCOTT13: This never gets old, does it?

Andy sat in front of the computer and ran his right hand over the stubble on his head. Even though he'd yet to shave his face, Andy had become an expert with a razor blade. Coach Ocampo had told him that a swimmer had to do every little thing to make himself quicker in the pool. Even a tenth of a second could be the difference between an Olympic medal and finishing back in the pack. So Andy made sure he didn't have hair on his head, or on his chest, or on his legs. If his skin was smooth, he'd glide through the water.

Superpuke, you're gonna have to learn, Andy thought. *We'll be doing you a favour.*

2 GETTING THERE

The quiet was broken by the sound of his mother calling from the kitchen. His bedroom rattled from his mom's deep, booming voice.

"Und-raassshhhhhhh," she yelled. She always used his full Hungarian name. Never "Andy" or "Andrew." Always András, pronounced with a long, hard *shhh* at the end, as if she wanted it to be followed with a moment of silence.

Andy opened the door, headed down a steep narrow staircase and made a right turn into the kitchen. A white tablecloth with embroidered flowers covered the kitchen table. Blue plates with floral designs hung from the wall.

His father sat at the far end of the table, in front of an open laptop.

"Kar-*chee*," Andy's mother said to his father. "Please put that computer away. Time to eat."

His father shut the laptop and laid it on an open seat next to him. "Six more weeks. I just checked."

"You check almost every hour of every day," Mrs. Kovacs snapped. "It doesn't change. You said 'it should be six more weeks' this morning."

"Sorry for living," Mr. Kovacs sighed. "It's just that the union is hopeful that new shifts might be added sooner than that."

"Well I am happy if you will be going back to work in six weeks," Andy's mom said as she ladled out some dark red stew into a bowl. "Because since the plant shutdown, you've been sitting here in this kitchen driving me nuts."

Mr. Kovacs smiled and pointed to his son. "You see? Till death do us part, huh? Can't wait to get rid of me!"

Mrs. Kovacs brought the bowl of *gulyás* to the table and placed it on the mat in front of Andy.

"There's an old Hungarian saying that the empty can makes the biggest noise. Your father makes a lot of noise. Complaining about this and that. András, you are lucky you are at school or at practice most of the time."

"So Andy," his father said as he tore off a piece of bread from a loaf that sat in the middle of the table. "How goes the swimming?" His father plunged the chunk of bread into the stew and popped it into his mouth.

"I'm swimming the time. I can make it to nationals."

His dad swallowed hard. "And where are these nationals this year?"

"Edmonton."

"Okay so, to help out with the travel, you'll have a bit of money saved from your job?"

"I hope so. I wanted to talk to Mr. Patel about some new shifts here and there."

"Good, good. Look, we'll be okay."

"But, Karcsi . . ." his mom said. "Have you seen his math marks? He needs to spend his spare time studying, not swimming more, not taking on more shifts. I finally remembered the password and checked the SchoolZone account the other day. His teacher said Andy is having a hard time. He doesn't pay attention!"

"I'll do better, Mom," said Andy. "I think Mr. Chalmers has it out for me. But I will get the mark up. You'll see."

WELCOME TO THE DUFFERIN-PEEL CATHOLIC DISTRICT SCHOOL BOARD'S SCHOOLZONE

Parent login:
Student: Kovacs, Andrew
MATHEMATICS (MID-TERM GRADE): 55
TEACHER: CHALMERS, SCOTT
COMMENTS: *Andy is still struggling with some of the concepts required in grade 9 mathematics. Part of the problem is Andy's constant inattention in class. He can't grasp the lessons if he's not paying attention to them. His attitude needs to change.*

***

Andy looked at the cover of *Galaxy Queen* No. 119. The heroine was wearing a black body suit with a blue cape flowing behind. She was falling from a red sky, blonde hair flowing. Her lips were cherry red.

"Stop staring, start sorting," said Mr. Patel as he looked up from the cash register where he'd been counting money.

"Sorry, Mr. Patel," Andy said. He took a pile of comics from the table and started sorting them on the new-release rack. He did the A titles first. *Agent 19*; *Alan Fine, P.I.*; *ARGH!*; *Armed Combat*; *Awesome Adventures*.

Mr. Patel smiled. "You are like a kid in a candy store."

"Oh, this is way better than a candy store."

Andy had been coming to Comic Relief since the store first opened on the second level of the Bramalea City Centre, the largest mall in town. When Mr. Patel put a "help wanted" sign in the window a couple of months ago, Andy thought he was dreaming. Could there be a better job for him?

For every comic-book fan, Wednesday was the best day of the week. That's when all the new comics were released. But to have them ready for Wednesday mornings, Mr. Patel and Andy stayed behind on Tuesday nights, after the store closed, to open the boxes and get the comics onto the shelves. And that meant Andy got to see the comics a day before most of the rest of world did. The job started out as a great way to preview the latest comics. Now he needed to save every cent from his paycheques to help pay for his trip to the Canadian Age Group Championships.

Andy finished putting the final few comics on to the new-release rack: *Weirdest Worlds*; *Yellow Planet; Zyzyk: Lord of the Dark Realm*. Meanwhile, Mr. Patel was behind the cash register, counting bills and sorting through receipts.

"Looks like you're going to be done before me," Mr. Patel said.

"Need any help with those?" Andy asked.

"Oh, no, I can't promote you to do the accounting just yet," Mr. Patel said. "I'll be fifteen minutes or so . . . then I'll lock up and we can both go."

"By the way," said Andy, "if there's anything else you need a hand with, I can take on some extra shifts."

Mr. Patel laughed. "Andy, it's June. And that means exam time for you. And then you have your practices. You surely don't have time for more shifts."

"I can fit them in, honest."

Nothing was more important than qualifying for nationals and getting to Edmonton.

3 THE NUMBERS

WELCOME TO THE OFFICIAL WEBSITE OF SWIM CANADA

RANKINGS: ONTARIO
100-metre freestyle (14-year-olds):
1. Kovacs, Andrew, COBRA, 56.21
2. Li, Mark, WHITBY, 56.65

"So, if you take the variable and place it on the other side of the equation . . ." Mr. Chalmers's voice trailed off. He looked to the back corner of the classroom, where Andy was sitting.

"Mr. Kovacs." Mr. Chalmers ran his hand over his close-cut afro. "What could be on your phone that is more interesting than what I am talking about right now?"

Andy looked up. His face was as red as the school sweater he wore. "Um, sir, I wasn't looking at my phone . . ."

"Oh, Mr. Kovacs." The teacher sighed and then slowly walked across the classroom toward Andy's desk.

"Really, don't make it harder for yourself. I can see you trying to hide it there under your bag. You thought you could watch it without me noticing. Problem is, you didn't take into consideration that the screen gives off a glow. Look, let me keep the phone to the end of class, even though you know about the rules against devices in the classroom. But lying might get you a trip to the office. Neither of us wants that."

"Okay," Andy stuttered, "I was just trying to get some math help."

Mr. Chalmers hurried his pace and snatched the smartphone from Andy's hand. He looked at the screen. "Yes, it looks like you were seeking help on the website for, let's see, swimming rankings. Congratulations, I see here that you are a better swimmer than you are a math student."

"Sir!" Andy croaked. "You can't look at the screen. Invasion of privacy."

Mr. Chalmers nodded, turned around and walked back to the front of the class with the phone in hand. "Yes, Andy, I suppose it is," he said. "And you can take the matter up with the principal if you'd like. But then I can also share your recent test scores with him."

Andy shrugged and looked down at his math textbook. "Okay, you win. Keep it and I won't say a thing. Sir."

At the front of the class, Mr. Chalmers talked about flipping equations. Andy tried to concentrate, but he couldn't stop thinking about how smoothing out his flip turns could shave a few more tenths of a second off his lap times.

Andy passed the next twenty minutes trying to focus on the numbers on the board. But he just kept writing the number 56 in his notebook.

At the end of class, Andy reclaimed his phone from Mr. Chalmers. Enalyn waited for him in the hallway.

"You do realize exams are just two weeks away?"

"It's okay," Andy said. "I'll do well enough in this class to squeak by."

"Squeak by, that's good enough for you? Really?"

"Aw, come on, En," Andy said as he trailed her toward the school cafeteria. They passed by the food lineup and right to one of the tables.

"Andy, I know you don't think school is all that important," Enalyn said as she sat down across from him.

Andy opened his notebook. Enalyn craned her neck to see.

"So instead of copying down equations, you just wrote 56 over and over?"

"It's the most important number in the world," Andy said. "I'm hungry. I'm going to go stand in line over there. Want anything?"

"I'll get my own when I'm ready," Enalyn said in an icy tone. "You know, when the exam comes in two weeks, I bet none of the answers to any of the questions will be 56."

"Well, maybe *one* of them." Andy smiled.

Enalyn shook her head. "You know, sometimes I don't know why I waste my time hanging out with you. You're '56 seconds this' and '56 seconds that.'"

"That's the time that'll get me to nationals," said Andy.

"And you've been swimming that time in practice for weeks now. So stop being so worried about your time and worry a little more about algebra."

Andy scratched his head. "Look, we have practice in the mornings, practice in the evenings. I also work a bit at the comic shop. It's hard to fit the homework in."

Enalyn put her hand on Andy's shoulder. "Look, I do the two-a-day practices, too. And I can still pull a decent grade."

Andy smiled. "Well, maybe you could give me some extra help?"

Enalyn's face reddened just a little. "Of course I'd help you. But you better take it seriously!"

@Just_Enalyn
@TheREALMiriamSaid Any tips on how to get faster?

@TheREALMiriamSaid
@Just_Enalyn In the pool? Practice, practice, practice.

@Just_Enalyn
@TheREALMiriamSaid But, I need to get better, as in, right away.

@TheREALMiriamSaid
@Just_Enalyn I'm sorry, @Just_Enalyn. There is no quick fix. It takes time.

4 SWIM MEET

@TigerShark
@MarkLi Just saw the latest rankings. Still NUMBER ONE!

@MarkLi
@TigerShark Rankings are nice. But all that matters is having the best time on race day.

The deck was crowded with swimmers.

Coach Ocampo walked over to Andy. "Pretty good turnout for our little invitational meet, huh? I think the Whitby Dolphins and the Mississauga swim club sent all of their best swimmers."

Coach Ocampo had arranged for two of the best swim teams in the Toronto region to come to Brampton for a Saturday invitational meet. On a table in the Earnscliffe lobby sat a trophy and some medals, sponsored by local businesses.

"I don't see him," said Andy.

"Oh, Mark Li?" asked Coach Ocampo. "I was just talking to Whitby's coach. He told me that Mark is here, all right. What, you worried about him or something?"

Then Andy saw him. Mark Li. Wearing what Andy thought was a silly-looking Dolphin swim cap on his head. *Who's afraid of a dolphin?* Andy wondered.

"I'm not worried about him," Andy said. "Every time I've raced him this year, I've won. And I'm usually a second or so faster."

"Well you just worry about yourself," said the coach. "Just worry about your form. This meet is about getting ready for provincials. Concentrate on your turns."

The provincials would be held at a long-course pool, 50 metres long, which was the Olympic size. But not all recreation centres were built to hold a pool that long, so COBRA, like many swim teams in the country, trained in a 25-metre pool, a short course. To swim a 100-metre race in an Olympic-size pool, a swimmer had to turn just once. In the short-course pool, it took four laps — and three turns — to do the same distance.

Andy nodded and then plunged into the pool.

Enalyn bobbed next to Andy. "All we're missing is squirt guns and noodles for it to look like a community-pool free swim. It's crazy here."

"Hey, aren't you racing soon?" Andy asked.

"Yup," nodded Enalyn. "My race is the first on the schedule."

"Well, you should tear it up — like you're Miriam Said or something."

"Andy, Miriam Said has set every provincial record she's ever had her eye on. I'll be happy to finish top three. Heck, if I ever got into the same pool as her, I'd be freaked out. She's going to be the best swimmer this country has ever produced."

"Well, if you make it to provincials, you'll be able to see her face-to-face."

Enalyn smacked her hand against the surface of the water, splashing Andy in the face. "Andy, can you stop with all of this? I said I'd be happy to finish top three today, maybe set a personal best."

Andy swam away and tried to focus on some kind of warm-up. He rotated his arms. But he couldn't stop thinking about what it would be like to beat Mark Li again.

★★★

"En, go! Faster, faster!"

Andy screamed. He pumped his fist. He jumped up and down on the deck. But he couldn't make Enalyn's breaststrokes any faster. She was in fifth place when she got to the first turn. She held the spot into the second and third lap, but then got passed by the swimmer in lane 1. She was now in sixth. Her arms pushed forward, shovelling the water from out in front of her. But she was a third of a length behind the swimmer in the lead.

By the fourth lap, Andy resigned himself to the fact that she would finish nowhere near the podium.

She held onto sixth spot.

Enalyn climbed out of the pool and ripped off her goggles and swim cap.

Andy walked over to her. Coach Ocampo had beaten him there.

"Your turns were awfully good," said the coach. "That's what you have to take from this. This meet is not the be-all and end-all. There are positives to take from this."

Andy noticed a couple of droplets on Enalyn's face moving downward from her eyes.

At least, with her face wet, you have to look real close to notice she's crying, he thought.

"Enalyn, um . . ." he started.

"It's okay, Andy, really." Enalyn took a deep breath and looked down. "Just go and get ready for your race."

Andy walked away. He felt a bit relieved because talking to a girl when she was crying was way too weird for him to handle. Andy tried to pay attention to the next race. The Eel was in a boys' breaststroke event. The Eel did pretty well — he finished second — but Andy had a hard time focusing. He kept thinking about how slow Enalyn had been.

I hope that never happens to me, Andy thought.

It was time for Andy to go to the blocks for his best event, the 100-metre freestyle. As the club's best swimmer, Andy had been entered into a bunch of events, but the 100-metre free was his favourite.

He was in lane 3. He saw that Mark Li had gotten onto the lane-5 block. Andy looked over to Mark, and waved.

Mark Li shrugged. "What's your problem?"

"Waving you goodbye," Andy said as he pulled down his silver goggles. "You know what a Tiger Shark's favourite meal is? Dolphin!"

The race-starter blew a whistle. The boys all got set on their blocks. Then the pop of the starter's gun. Andy plunged into the water. *One. Two. Three. Breathe.* His pace was strong. He felt like a predator cutting through the water; instead of arms and legs, he had razor-sharp fins.

He got to the second turn and exploded off the wall. He pushed off so hard, it was like he had TNT in his ankles. In the water, his ears filled with a *zinnggg* sound.

He came out of the third turn and headed for home. He saw the wall coming up toward him. He stretched, stretched . . . and the race was done. He popped out of the water and glanced toward lane 5. Mark Li wasn't at the wall yet! He was still a stroke away from the finish.

Andy pumped his fist into the air. Finally, Mark Li hit the wall, followed by six other swimmers. Li's head popped into the air.

"Hey, they need a calendar to time you, not a stop-watch!" Andy called out toward Mark. "But silver's still a nice colour. You should do up your trophy room in silver. I can help you with that!"

5 PROVING YOURSELF

Andy and some of his teammates sat in the men's change room. Andy had three medals — two gold and one bronze — around his neck. He'd won the 100- and 200-metre freestyle races. He also anchored the relay team, but his best efforts couldn't improve COBRA's third-place finish — out of three teams.

Andy tried as hard as he could to suppress a smile as the new guy walked in, soaking wet. After the meet was done, the COBRA members who hadn't competed had gone into the water. They'd also been put in charge of putting away the lane ropes.

"Hey, Superpuke, good on you," Andy said, loud enough for his voice to echo off every corner of the change room. "You are maybe the best clean-up guy in team history. And your penmanship on the registration forms? Fantastic."

Some of the other members of the team snickered. *It's too bad Enalyn can't see this*, thought Andy. *This might cheer her up.*

The new guy shuffled to an open slot on the bench as the rest of his teammates laughed.

"Okay, I'm sorry. That was mean," Andy said. He walked over to where his open gym bag sat on the bench and pulled out a black swim cap with COBRA emblazoned on it in yellow. He then brought it over to the new guy.

"Here. Try this on," Andy said.

"Thanks," the new guy said. And then he pressed the swim cap over his head, fitting it tightly over his blond locks. Andy had to look away to stop himself from laughing.

The new guy looked at Andy. "By the way, you've called me Superpuke for the last week or so. My name is Zach."

Andy looked hard at Zach. "Hey, look. Don't feel too bad about the nickname thing. We all get nicknames. As you know, I'm the Tiger Shark, Jamie over there is the Electric Eel, Scott is the Stingray. And as you know, well, you're . . . you're . . . Superpuke."

Andy began to laugh. He slid off the bench and fell to the floor. He was laughing so hard, he couldn't get the rest of what he wanted to say out of his mouth. So Jamie, the Eel, stood up.

"Hey, Zach. Do you like the new cap?"

Zach simply put his hands to his head.

"Well," said the Eel, "you know that swimmers don't want a lot of hair, right? Slows us down. We all thought your hair was too long. So, well, we fixed your cap before we gave it to you."

"What? What?" Zach opened his eyes wide.

Andy's laugh had turned into a series of hacking coughs. It was one of the oldest pranks in the book, but it was a beauty. At least Andy thought so. Before Zach got to the dressing room, Andy had smeared hair remover inside the cap.

"Don't worry," the Eel smiled. "That heat you're feeling right now is only your scalp burning. At least that stuff washes out fast."

"You . . . you . . ." Zach tore the cap off his head and dashed around the corner. The rest of the guys on the team heard the hiss of the shower.

"It burns!" They heard Zach's voice echoing. "My hair! It's coming out in patches! I'll kill you guys! All of you!"

★★★

Andy sat in one of the comfy-but-worn pink chairs on the second floor of the Chinguacousy library, located across the parking lot from the City Centre. His phone lay in front of him on the table.

Enalyn sat across from him at the study table.

On the desk in between them lay pages and pages of equations and notes.

"So at practice today you looked a bit quicker,"

Andy said.

"Yeah, maybe a quarter-second. Still not nearly fast enough," Enalyn said. "And enough with the swimming talk. Exams are coming up fast and you want to ace it, right? Well, here are the notes. Here's how you move the variable to the other side of the equation, and then you can work backward to . . ."

"Work backward?"

"Didn't you follow any of this in Mr. Chalmers's class?" Enalyn hissed, her voice threatening to rise above a whisper. "It's not that hard. You just take the variable here and then move it. And now, instead of adding, you're subtracting."

"Enalyn," Andy said, looking down at the worn carpet. "There's only a couple of weeks before exams, then there's only a couple till we go to provincials. You don't have much time left. You need to get faster. Take what happened last weekend at the meet as a wake-up call. You can't let that happen again."

"Andy!" Enalyn yelled. All around the library, heads swivelled and stared at her and Andy. She turned red and gave Andy a cold stare. She gathered her notes from the table. "Andy, it's clear you don't want to study. Why bother? We're done here."

"Hey!"

Enalyn shoved the papers into her backpack, got up and rushed down the stairs, leaving Andy alone at the study table.

Andy grabbed his phone from the table and began to text.

What?

Leave me alone.

Why?

I'm not good enough for you, am I? All you care about is time.

Andy was about to send another message to Enalyn, but his phone buzzed. He'd received a text message from the Eel.

Hey, did you get the e-mail from coach? Ha!

Andy swiped over to his e-mail.

FROM: coachOcampo@COBRA.ca
TO: TigerShark@gmail.com, slipperyeel@hotmail.com
SUBJECT: Suspension

Gentlemen:

Look, I know and you know the hair-remover thing is the oldest trick in the book. But I've got to do something. You should know, the new kid's got guts. He decided to shave his head after what you guys did to him. And he did it without coming to me, and before his parents found out. He just told them that he needed to be faster and needed to lose the hair. He didn't mention the prank at all to them.

So, cut him some slack now. He's been initiated. Don't come to practice tomorrow. I'm going to suspend you all for the day.

COACH

Andy's phone buzzed again. Another e-mail had arrived in his inbox. And it was from the coach, but this one was addressed only to him.

FROM: coachOcampo@COBRA.ca
TO: TigerShark@gmail.com
SUBJECT: Enalyn

Andy, I know you talk to Enalyn and all that. Anyways, she sent me an e-mail earlier saying that she wanted to quit. Do you know anything about this?

6 SLOW DOWN

@MarkLi

You still talking, @TigerShark? Can't wait to wipe that smile off your face.

@TigerShark

@MarkLi you are soooo brave on Twitter. Soooo tough. Where was that at the meet, huh?

@MarkLi

I'm not gonna pop off at a meet like an idiot . . . like @TigerShark does.

@TigerShark

Can't wait to beat @MarkLi again at provincials. Does he need a head start?

@MarkLi

I will beat you when it counts, @TigerShark. See you at provincials.

The water rushed against Andy's face. He breathed out of his nose, hard, as he rotated through his flip turn. Blowing the air out helped keep the water from rushing up his nostrils. He pushed off the wall and headed back in the direction he'd just come from.

I'm slow this morning, he thought. *Really slow. Like, Mark Li slow.*

When Andy surfaced to take a gulp of air, he heard the coach yelling.

"Andy, faster! Faster!"

He didn't need the coach to tell him that. He knew he needed to pick up the pace. He tried to find an extra gear to make his legs kick harder and faster.

He got to the wall and surfaced.

The coach stood on the deck, stopwatch in his hand. "That's like, wow. Almost 57.5 seconds. What's up with you?"

Andy slapped the water. He tore the swim cap and goggles off his head and threw them onto the deck. "You didn't need to tell me my time, Coach. I could tell."

Zach was in the next lane, treading water next to the Eel.

"If Tiger Shark swims any slower, well, that's like a girl's time," said the Eel. "Or worse, it could be close to your times, Superpuke."

"How did he know that he was that slow?" Zach asked. Both he and the Eel kept treading water, but raised their arms out of the air — an exercise meant to build stronger legs and endurance.

They treaded for 60 seconds, working so hard that it was too tough to talk. Then the Eel floated over to the edge of the deep end and grabbed ahold of the wall. "You'll get it after you've been doing this a while. Every swimmer knows if he's faster or slower than his usual pace. Even if you're just a second off, you know it."

Andy hopped out onto the deck. He then dropped and did twenty-five push-ups.

"Wow, push-ups without asking," said the coach. "You really must be pissed off there, Andy."

Andy didn't say a word.

When Andy grunted through his final push-up, the coach leaned forward and whispered. "So, did you talk to Enalyn?"

"No. She's not talking to me, at all."

The coach looked at his watch and then blew his whistle, which echoed through Earnscliffe Pool. "Okay, okay, that's it for the day! You've got a few minutes, everyone, before the pool opens to the public for lane swims!"

Some of the swimmers got out of the pool. A few of them finished the last of their laps.

The Eel and Zach joined Andy on deck.

"What's up with you?" the Eel asked Andy.

"Stupid math exam is all over my head. I've got

to write that thing later today. I hardly slept last night. Enalyn was going to help me with it, but she hasn't talked to me since, well . . ."

"She quit," said the Eel. "Not even in class?"

"Nope. I tried passing her notes and stuff. She crumples them up. She won't sit near me in the cafeteria. So I'm here struggling with math on my own."

"What about asking your mom and dad?" asked Zach.

"Okay, who asked you?" said Andy.

"Whoa," said the Eel, placing his palms down. "Easy, Andy. Superpuke, I mean, Zach here, he's okay. Remember that he didn't rat us out, right? He took his initiation like a champ. And he's got a point. If math is killing you, why don't you ask your mom and dad?"

Andy shook his head. "If my parents think I'm struggling, they might tell me that I need to stop swimming! The way I look at it is this: I've just got to get through the exam. The final marks won't come out for a couple more weeks, and I'll already have gone to provincials."

"And when the marks *do* come out?" asked Zach.

"Well, my parents are kinda hopeless when it comes to the SchoolZone account. My mom checks it maybe two or three times a semester, max. I had to help them set it up, so I have the password. If I keep checking it, I can see the report card before they do. I can check off that it's been seen. And maybe they won't remember to check on the report card till after I make it to nationals."

"They're *that* hopeless at computers?" asked Zach.

"I remember the bank teller asking my mom why she goes into the branch to pay the bills, when she could do it online. My mom said something like 'you should thank me for keeping you in your job.' My dad still reads the *Brampton Guardian* — not online, the real paper, all opened up on the kitchen table, and underlines the stuff he finds interesting in red pen —"

"Okay, let's get you out of this rut," the Eel interrupted. "Flutterboard surfing!"

The Eel hurled the flutterboard into the pool. It splashed and then floated. There was applause from Andy's teammates and even a chant of "Tiger Shark! Tiger Shark!"

Andy shrugged, made a dash for the edge of the pool and jumped. He grabbed the rope that dangled from the ceiling. He looked down between his feet as he swung out over the water. There was the flutterboard, bobbing up and down. Andy dropped. He hit the board.

And he surfed. And surfed. Farther than he'd gone before. Farther than he'd seen anyone go before. Instead of sinking, he kept riding the flutterboard that was skipping up and down on the waves.

When he finally sank, he was in the shallow end. He'd almost done the whole length of the pool.

Then he heard Zach. "I got that all! I got it all on my phone! The whole run!"

And then he heard the coach. "Zachary! No cell phones in the pool area! Rules are rules!"

★★★

Andy sat in one of the desks set up in rows in the school gym. The white dress shirt that was part of his uniform made him itch all over. His red school cardigan was draped over the back of his chair. His math exam was on the desk in front of him.

Andy looked down to the first page. He looked at question one. He exhaled deeply. This isn't so bad! I can figure out the answer here. All I have to do is move the variable, like Enalyn showed me . .

He scribbled down the answers to the first three questions. He knew he'd got them all right, and it had only taken a couple of minutes!

He flipped to the next page — and his grin disappeared. The blood rushed to his face. The questions may as well have been written in Klingon. These were word problems, which would force him to combine fractions. There were variables. And, worst yet, at the end of every question on the page, he was asked to "show his work."

Andy placed numbers and letters into what looked like orderly rows. He tried his best to approximate "working through" an answer, even if he wasn't sure if the solution was going to be correct.

He flipped ahead through the next four pages of the exam. There were two pages of multiple-choice questions. Even though the word problems were a total bomb, he thought that if he could get lucky choosing a, b, c or d, he might squeeze out a 50.

Then he took a deep breath. *Andy, the only math that matters is . . . what's less than 56 seconds? You let Enalyn get you all worked up about math. Then she quit on you. She couldn't take the pressure of swimming anymore. And you're on your own. But you still have the 100 metres. You can ace that. Who cares about math?*

He kept thinking about how he needed to refocus on his swimming as he randomly filled in bubbles: *a* bubbles, *b* bubbles, *c* bubbles and *d* bubbles.

7 GOING VIRAL

Andy crashed through the doors and outside into a hot, humid summer afternoon. From there, he could see smoke coming from the car plant where his dad had worked — and hoped to work again. He took off his red cardigan and stuffed it into his bag. He undid two buttons near the collar of his dress shirt.

He turned on his phone. As soon as the start-up screen faded, his phone started to buzz and shake. Again. And again. And again.

Andy looked at the Twitter icon.

That can't be right, he thought.

The number 471 appeared in a red circle, set on top of the Twitter icon.

Andy tapped the icon, and the blue Twitter screen came into view. In that short span of time, he saw the number of notifications jump from 471 to 483.

What?

He looked through his feed.

@SuperGeek17
RT Check out this video: Pool surfing courtesy @TigerShark.

@TheBramptonian
Who is @TigerShark? Is this even a sport?!!!!!

@DaveDean33
Check out this vid posted by @ZachAttack: Some guy named @TigerShark. Blew me away, dude.

@MarkLi
What's wrong with you people? @TigerShark is the worst. He's the absolute WORST.

His phone kept buzzing every few seconds. Notifications flashed on his screen. Not just on Twitter. But on Facebook, too.

Andy Kovacs, Mike D'Amico has commented on a post you're tagged in.

Andy switched over from Twitter to Facebook. He saw dozens of comments under a video. The video was posted by . . . Zach Ferguson.

Superpuke did this.

Andy clicked on the video. He watched as he came into view, swinging over the surface of Earnscliffe Pool.

Then he dropped, carrying momentum from the swing. And he shot across the pool, somehow keeping steady on top of the tiny flutterboard. He rode and rode across the pool.

Likes: 267
Shares: 48

Graham Jackson
Wow, LOL. Is that a sport? So crazy!

Jasmine Mohamed
If it's not a sport it should be.

Raymond Chang
The dude's handle is @TigerShark on Twitter.

Marcos Mark
I could do this. Lame.

James Pearce
Boyeeeeeeeeee

Mike Harden
LOL Splash-down

Raymond Chang
Seriously, you gotta follow this guy @TigerShark on

Twitter he's been having this twitterfight with another guy for days and days so classic.

Maria Jackson-Haynes
Holy crap that's awesome but yeah what's with that MarkLi dude who hates him so much?

And the list went on. And Andy's phone kept buzzing. And buzzing.

What do you know? Andy thought. *I'm going viral. And all because of Superpuke.*

***

Andy lay in his bed. He looked up at the ceiling. His phone was in his hands. He'd been turning it over and over. He had just finishing playing his fifth Connect Four game. He'd crushed all the candy he'd ever wanted to crush.

He started to text, erased it, and then put down the phone again. He'd had to turn off the notification features just so he'd get peace.

"András, come down for dinner in five minutes!" his mom yelled from the kitchen.

Andy began another text and deleted it. And then he began another. He finished it, hit send and regretted it immediately.

Enalyn? U there? Did u see the video?

For a minute, there was nothing. Then Andy saw the three dots in the bubble. The message appeared.

I can't believe you.

Another bubble.

You can't bring yourself to say anything to me, then you go viral and you want to talk?

Another bubble.

Go away!

Andy put the phone down and walked downstairs to the kitchen. His mom had made cabbage rolls, served with sauerkraut and sausages. He scooped up a roll and put it on his plate. He then put two solid tablespoons of sour cream on top.

"Hey, leave some sour cream for us!" His dad smiled and playfully punched his son in the arm.

His mom sat down across from Andy. "So, how'd the exam go today?"

"Fine," Andy said, not looking up from his food.

"Well, I'm just a bit concerned. I thought that Enalyn girl was going to help you with math."

"Well, you see, Mom, I didn't see her."

Andy's dad looked at his mom. "Really, leave the boy alone. He is doing fine, I am sure. He has to swim or else, *poof*! There goes nationals. And we'll have been saving up our money for nothing!"

"You know what I'd like?" his mom said. "For Andy to speed into grade 10. No problems, no issues. The schools here are so soft, so even if there was a problem, he could probably skate right through, I guess."

If only Mom knew, Andy said.

His dad sighed and took another bite of food.

"But you didn't answer one thing," Andy's dad said as he peeled a strand of sauerkraut from his chin. "This Enalyn girl."

"She's busy," Andy said.

"Girl trouble, already," his dad said.

"By the way, Dad," Andy said, changing the subject. "I'm going to bike to the City Centre after tonight's practice. Going to meet Mr. Patel after closing to go through the shipment for tomorrow."

His mom made a harrumphing sound.

"Look, Mom, I need the shifts. Every shift I get helps the send-Andy-to-nationals fund, right?"

"As long as you don't spend the money on those idiotic comic books and those dolls."

"Action figures, Mom. *Action figures*. Not dolls. And I haven't bought any for months."

"See?" Andy's dad laughed. "And you worry that our son isn't responsible? He's growing out of those dolls with the tight pyjamas on them!"

8 CHANGING THE GAME

Andy had just sorted through dozens of new comic releases. Hundreds of issues had been organized alphabetically on racks near the entrance of Comic Relief. Mr. Patel was in the office, looking at the order sheets, making sure nothing was missing from the shipment.

Andy gazed out into the mall. All of the shops were closed, and a security guard walked through the empty food court that was just across from Comic Relief. Near the food court was a set of up and down escalators; the steps were moving, but no one was riding.

Andy still felt a chill every time his phone buzzed. It had been hours since the video was posted, but his notification numbers went up by hundreds every time he checked. He had gone from having 230 followers on Twitter to 17,656 followers, at last count.

Andy checked his Twitter account again. Now at 18,114 followers. Wait. Four more notifications.

"Andy?"

He looked up from the screen and saw that Mr.

Patel was standing over him.

"Sorry, Mr. Patel. We ready to go?"

"Um, no," said Mr. Patel, pointing to a pair of boxes behind the racks. "I was going to ask you why you didn't unpack those two boxes of action figures. Did you need to take a break?"

Andy looked across the floor. *Where did those boxes come from? Were they there the whole time?*

"Andy, I'm not totally out of touch, for an old man." Mr. Patel shrugged. "I know that you've just become the most famous man in Canada. In fact, I was on the Sports Channel's website, and they actually had a link to that video you're in. But I see that you're on the phone. I bet you're checking to see just how famous you've become. And then there's a couple of unpacked boxes right in front of you."

Andy put away his phone, picked up an X-Acto knife and got to work. He slashed open the first box. "I promise, Mr. Patel, this will take no more than fifteen minutes to get these all out on display."

Mr. Patel checked his watch. "Good. You think you can stay off the Twitter feed till it's done?"

Andy put the action figures on the shelves and resisted the urge to put one of them on hold. He had an employee discount: 20 per cent off! But he thought about nationals and the money he would need to get to Edmonton. He made a promise to himself. If he medalled at nationals, he'd reward himself when he got back.

If only there was a way that I could raise the money for nationals and still have money for comics and stuff, he thought. Andy then waved goodbye to Mr. Patel.

"Goodnight, superstar," laughed Mr. Patel. "Don't let the fame go to your head. I don't want to lose an employee because he's in the most popular video in the world."

Andy thought about what Mr. Patel had just said as the shop owner unlocked the gate so they could slide out into the mall.

"That's it!" Andy bellowed.

"What?" said Mr. Patel.

"Of course, what a great idea!" Andy then sprinted down the escalator steps, leaving Mr. Patel behind. He did a one-eighty, which took him out to the parkade, close to the City Centre's bus terminal. His bike was locked there.

He got on and pedalled hard, going across the bus terminal and out onto Clark Boulevard. He pushed the pedals as if he were in the Tour de France. He wanted to get to his computer as quickly as he could. He turned right onto Bramalea Road, then rode till he got to Darras Court, the townhouse complex where he lived.

He walked into his house. His parents were watching TV. He said hi, got a couple of nods in return and sped up the stairs to his bedroom. He sat in front of his computer, hit the keys and the screen came to life.

He got on the Internet and found the bookmark

for SchoolZone. He had his dad's password: ferencvaros. That was the name of his father's favourite soccer team. Andy knew that his dad used it as his password for pretty well anything that required a password.

Andy logged in and saw there were no new reports under his student profile. Then he went to account information. He changed the primary contact e-mail from maria_kovacs@gmail.com to kovacs1356@hotmail.com. Any updates about his student profile would now go to the dummy e-mail he'd set up earlier that afternoon. His mom would still be able to access SchoolZone and see his grades, but she wouldn't be getting any e-mail reminders.

Satisfied with his work, Andy went into the browser history and deleted the last session. He knew his parents were fairly computer illiterate, but he couldn't be too careful.

Now, Andy rubbed his hands together.

Thanks, Mr. Patel. You're right. I am going to use my fame to get rich. Or at least pay for my trip.

FundMyProject.com
SEND TIGER SHARK to NATIONALS!

My name is Andy Kovacs, also known as "Tiger Shark." You might recognize me from this video of me surfing across a pool. I'm a swimmer from Brampton, Ontario, Canada, and I hope to swim at the Olympics. I am the fastest swimmer in Ontario in the 100-metre freestyle for my age group.

But the nationals this year are in Edmonton, which is a far way away. Plane rides are expensive, and my family isn't rich. My dad works hard, but he's waiting for his factory to reopen. My mom does her best with her part-time jobs. But I could use some help. So, what I am offering is for you to be a part of history. If you help fund my trip to the nationals, you can tell the world you helped a future Olympian.

Here it is: Donate $5, and I will tweet out my thanks! Tell the world you are awesome.

$10: I will e-mail you regular updates on my progress and make you part of the Tiger Shark Club.

$100 or more: If you are in the Toronto area, I will give you or someone you choose a swimming lesson. It'll have to be unofficial, though.

COMMENTS

Dan Hardy

Seems like a cool project. I'll toss in five bucks. Good luck, kid.

Maurice Dumars

Shout-out from Etobicoke! My mom says that you have to keep chasing your dreams. Big dreams. Good luck to you. I think I can scrape up five bucks.

Mark Li

You haven't EVEN GONE TO PROVINCIALS yet and you're trying to make money off it? I am gonna KICK YOUR ASS at provincials. I really hope you don't qualify so you'll to have to go back and refund the money you've raised. I can't believe people would be DUMB enough to pitch in to this. I cannot wait to wipe that smile off your face!

9 LANE SWIM

The school year was over. Now, with no classes during the day, Andy got some afternoon shifts at Comic Relief. After each shift, he biked over to Earnscliffe Pool and paid the fee to take part in the public lane swim. He needed to get faster. He thought that maybe, without any of his teammates watching, he could rediscover his groove.

For two weeks, it went like this. Work. Lane swim. Then he dried off, left the pool, got a snack and came back an hour later for his practice.

With just a week left to go till the summer long-course provincials, Andy had only one goal: to swim the 100 metres in 56 seconds. He had to get back in that rhythm.

Before walking into the dressing room for the Friday afternoon lane swim, Andy fished his phone from his pocket and checked on the status of his funding drive. He had a couple of weeks to go till his campaign ended.

FUNDS PLEDGED: $305
Supporters: 45

In the last 48 hours, I've only gone from 300 bucks to 305 bucks, thought Andy. *Well, better than nothing. Might pay for part of a plane ticket.*

As he left the men's change room and walked out onto the pool deck, he saw a new lifeguard patrolling the perimeter of the pool, a neon-green whistle-chain around her neck.

Enalyn.

Her eyes met Andy's, and then she looked away.

Andy approached her. "Enalyn? You work here now?"

"Andy, we're not talking."

"I'm a swimmer. And it looks like you're a lifeguard now. So if I ask you something, you have to talk to me."

Enalyn pointed to the wall. "The life jackets are over there. There's a life preserver on the other wall. Call out if you realize you're drowning. I'll come to help you, eventually."

"When did you get this job?"

"I'm sorry, sir. That's not a life-saving question. That's a personal question."

"C'mon Enalyn." Andy waited for Enalyn to respond. She didn't. She was looking over Andy's shoulder toward the pool.

"Um, I think, well, I think I might have bombed

that math exam," Andy mumbled.

Enalyn didn't move her head, but her eyes moved toward Andy, and then rolled. "That's a surprise," she said drily.

"I could have used your help."

"So I guess you really want to have this conversation, huh?"

"Yeah," Andy nodded.

"Okay, I'll break my vow of silence about talking to you. You say you could have used my help? You sure didn't act like it. You were too busy talking about yourself and your times and your swimming. Anything but what you needed to focus on."

"Yeah, well . . ."

Enalyn raised her hand. "I wasn't finished. You wanted me to talk to you? Well I'm talking now. And you've got to listen. You just used the study session as an excuse to rail on me about my times, even though I told you over and over not to. You're supposed to be my friend, and all you did was make me feel even worse about myself. And to think I had a huge crush on you, once."

Enalyn walked away and climbed up the ladder to the high lifeguard chair.

Crush? Andy thought. *What*?

"I decided I wasn't going to let anyone ruin the fact that, deep down inside, I like being at the pool. So I dropped out of the team and finished the lifesaver courses. Here I am. Summer job. But why are you here during public swim?"

"I've been slow. I need to get it back. Putting the time in to do some extra work . . . And, um, a crush?"

"I'm sure you'll be fine," she said. "And as for the crush thing, I was speaking in past tense."

"You could have done some extra laps, too," Andy said. "And maybe got your times down . . ."

"Andy! Maybe you should get in the pool. And really, don't get into any trouble out there, because I'm no longer undecided if I would jump in and rescue you. I wouldn't."

★★★

Andy sat at the dinner table across from his parents.

"Dad?" Andy asked, as he scooped out another spoonful of yellow bean soup and shovelled it into his mouth. "When you get in trouble with Mom, what's the best way to apologize?"

His mother laughed. "Your father doesn't know how to apologize."

"Not true," said Mr. Kovacs. "You have to pick your spot. Sometimes, even if you know exactly what you want to say, you need to know that the other person is going to listen to you."

"Your father waits to pick his spots, all right. Maybe in a couple of years or so, he'll apologize for mixing the colours and whites in the laundry. All the rainbow colours on the white sheets and shirts!"

Andy shook his head. "You know, neither of you are being much help."

"Okay," his mother laughed. "I will help. Don't ask your father. Ask me instead."

"Well?" Andy's voice trailed off.

"Chances are, the person is hoping you'll come back and want to talk to them."

"What if that person keeps telling you to go away?"

"Well, maybe you're not sending the right message. Maybe that person needs to see that you actually feel bad about whatever's gone on between you. Maybe you should just tell Enalyn three words. *I* and *am* and *sorry*."

"Why do you think it's Enalyn?"

"Oh, Andy, your parents might be getting older, but we're not senile yet."

***

Andy texted.

I. Am. Sorry.

Then, for good measure.

Really, I am. No jokes.

You were right. I needed help in math.

And I shouldn't have bugged you about your swim times.

Andy waited ten minutes. Then a half hour. The phone didn't buzz. After an hour, he put it down.

Well so much for your advice, Mom, he thought.

Andy got up and went downstairs. He flipped the TV on to one of his favourite superhero shows, *The Invisible Spy*. During one of the ad breaks, there was a trailer for the new *Galaxy Queen* movie. Andy noticed how much the moviemakers had changed Galaxy Queen's costume. In the comic, the character wore a body suit, but the Hollywood actress was dressed only in a tiny black bikini. The only thing they'd kept from the comic was the blue cape.

Andy's gawking was interrupted by a collection of buzzing and beeping sounds.

My phone! he thought. *I left it in my room!*

Andy raced upstairs to get to the phone before the call went to voice mail. He dashed into his room and snatched the phone so fast, he didn't have time to check the caller display.

"Hello?" he said.

"You really are a moron," came Enalyn's voice.

"What?"

"If you're going to apologize to someone, don't do it over text message. Call them. Say it in person."

"Oh."

"So, Andy, is there something you wanted to tell me?"

"Well, yeah, well . . . um . . ."

"Spit it out or I'm hanging up."

"Okay . . . Okay! I am sorry. Enalyn, really."

"Now was that so hard?"

"No, and I just wanted to say . . ."

"Andy, wait, don't say anything. I just want to savour this apology. I'm replaying it in my head, you saying 'I am sorry' in that sorta pathetic tone of voice."

"Aw, En . . ."

"Do you admit that sometimes you need help?"

"Yes!"

"Okay, I've been watching your laps. Your entries are all wrong there. They're way too deep."

"I know. Like the coach says, 'pretend you're diving into a puddle.' Coach has been giving me crap about it."

"I can see you're so worried about your entries. You're like a robot out there. Don't be so tense."

"Well, it's hard not to be tense when you're being watched by some lifeguard who hates you."

"Oh, Andy, I don't hate you. Wait. That's a lie. I did hate you just a little bit. Okay, a lot."

"And . . ."

"There's an old song that my mom has on her iPad. It has a line where the singer jokes about smashing someone in the head. By some band called The Smiths.

They're sorta good but I can never tell my mom that."

"Never heard of them. But do you want to smash my mouth?"

"I did. But now, I'm going to try to help you. Again. And this is the part where you tell me you'd really like it if I would go to Hamilton to watch you swim at the summer championships."

"Um, yeah."

"You're really bad at this, aren't you?"

"Yeah."

10 PROVINCIALS

The van that Coach Ocampo rented stuttered, stopped, started, stuttered, started, slowed, sped up and slowed again in the thick traffic.

"Coach, it's a good thing we got off to such an early start from Brampton," said the Eel, "because we were able to squeeze in this nice little tour of Hamilton from all your wrong turns."

The van finally pulled off the street and into a driveway that led to the McMaster University campus. Coach Ocampo had his phone perched on the dash.

"I think the parking lot closest to the pool is . . . hang a left, a right . . . there!" he said.

"Or you could just follow those other two vans coming in from that other street," said the Eel, who sat right in front of Andy. "Looks like they're going to the same place we are."

"Right!" said the coach. "We're almost there! Ontario Summer Long-Course Championships! Are we ready?"

Andy looked out the window. He knew he was ready. Over the last week, his form had returned. His entries were shallow and quick. His shoulders were rotating. His strokes were even. He was gliding through the water.

As they got out of the van and walked through the parking lot, Andy knew that his teammates and coach were still talking, but he couldn't hear them. All he could think about was getting off the blocks and into the pool — about swimming the race of his life.

He walked through the doors and into the aquatic centre. He ambled down the staircase that bisected the stands and strode onto the pool deck. He took a right turn into the change room. There were dozens of other swimmers in there, and they stopped when he walked in.

He knew many of them from earlier races. He'd beaten them before. He knew that if he swam as fast as he could, there was no way anyone there could beat him in his event — 100-metre freestyle.

I am the Tiger Shark, he thought.

He changed and went to the warm-up pool. It felt as if he could leave his body and look down on himself as he swam in the lane. He could see that his pace was perfect, that his strokes were true. The water parted for him. His kicks were strong, but not violent.

He paused only to look up toward the stands. And he saw lots of swimmers in the seats, talking with their coaches, talking with their parents. A man, though, sat alone in the top row. His head was shaved. He wore a red Swim Canada jacket. Andy recognized him. Travis Holloway! Canadian gold medalist at the Olympics — now the head coach of the Canadian swim program.

There was a din coming from the stands. But somehow, out of the chorus of voices, Andy could hear his named being called out. He looked toward the far end of the seats, and there was Enalyn, sitting next to his parents.

"You, Andy! I see you!" called Enalyn. "Now do what you've been doing all week!"

Andy got out of the pool. His event would come soon. His race was near the start of the schedule.

There were swimmers gathered on the deck. On their swim caps, Andy saw the names of many of the best swim clubs in the province: Toronto Swim Club, Whitby Dolphins, Etobicoke Swim Club and the Ottawa Kingfish.

Ottawa Kingfish! Andy thought. That meant *she* was here. Miriam Said must be nearby.

A small crowd had gathered around a TV camera in the far corner of the deck. Andy pushed through the arms, heads and shoulders. In the middle of the hubbub was Miriam Said. Her eyes were deep brown, shining brightly. Her perfect teeth were as white as the smiles in toothpaste commercials. A few strands of her curly black hair strayed from underneath a bright orange swim cap; on it, the Kingfish logo was featured in blue script. She wore a long robe that covered her swimsuit.

That cap kinda makes her head look like a can of orange juice, Andy thought. *And what's with the robe?* It looked strange in the middle of all the almost-naked bodies of the other swimmers.

The air was full of questions coming from the kids who surrounded the province's most famous swimmer.

"Miriam, are you gonna set another record today?"

"Do you think you'll be the best in the world one day?"

"Shut up! You're crowding her!"

Andy dashed back to the men's change room. He went to his stall and unlocked the door. He reached into his pants pocket and fished out his phone. He opened the Twitter app.

@TigerShark

Just saw @TheREALMiriamSaid on deck at OSLCC!

It only took about a minute before a response appeared.

@MarkLi

Did @TigerShark tell @TheREALMiriamSaid about how he's a douche?

Eight girls lined up on the blocks. They were ready for the first preliminary race for fourteen-year-old girls. Andy looked up at Enalyn in the stands. How could she stand watching? If she were only a couple of seconds faster, she would have been in this event.

The beep went off and the girls went into the pool. There were splashes and waves as the eight racers dashed to the other end, hit the wall and then turned back in the direction they'd come from. The first girl hit the wall to finish the race.

On the board came the winner's time: 59.67 seconds!

A boy next to Andy nudged him. "Holy crap, that's slow."

Andy knew it didn't matter who actually won the preliminary heats. A swimmer just needed to post one of the eight quickest heat times to earn a spot in tomorrow's final — that was the race for all the marbles.

"Aw, give it a break," Andy said to the swimmer next to him. "Look at Miriam Said. She's swimming later today, and she's the biggest attraction here."

"Darn right, she's a big attraction," said the boy, who had LESLIEVILLE emblazoned on his swim cap. As he spoke, another Leslieville swimmer joined them.

"I've heard of you," the other Leslieville swimmer said to Andy. "You have that video on YouTube."

"Yeah, I recognize you now!" the first Leslieville kid said. "You call yourself Tiger Shark. Ha! You've never been to nationals, and you think you're some kinda shark? Are you *that* dangerous in the pool? That's cocky!"

Andy felt like jumping into the water and not coming up again. He recognized this pair — they were both from Leslieville's U-16 relay team that had won several meets this year. Andy thought that either one of them could pick him up and throw him across the length of the pool. Their shoulders were as wide as the body building ads Andy saw in the comics.

The first swimmer continued. "You may have some big reputation, but you're still a newbie. Maybe you're a big deal with COBRA, whatever the hell club that is, but you're new meat here. And if you want anyone to take you — and that nickname, what a joke — seriously, well we all know rookies gotta do their initiations. And I'm not talking about something stupid like hair remover in a swim cap. After all, your head is already shaved. What's the point?"

Andy thought that he could simply walk away. He didn't need to listen to these guys. He could go swim a few laps in the practice pool. But he didn't do that. He stayed in the same spot — after all, what was the point of running from two Hulk look-alikes?

The first Leslieville swimmer said, "Yo, Tiger Shark, you were talking about how awesome Miriam Said is?"

"Yeah."

"Well, we all know later tonight she's gonna win her

heat, easy. And, well, not only is she fast, but she is, well . . ."

"Hot," Andy finished the thought.

"Right. And I bet you aren't man enough to go up there and be the first to run out there and plant a big kiss on her when she gets out of the pool."

"That's it?" Andy shrugged. "That's all you want me to do? To kiss Miriam Said?"

"Yup," said the Leslieville swimmer. "She's the biggest name here. She's the hottest girl here. And I bet when you get anywhere near her, you'll choke. You'll look like an idiot and we'll all get a laugh. Initiation done."

"What? Not man enough?" The second Leslieville swimmer jabbed his finger into Andy's chest. "We saw you talking to that girl up in the stands. Is she your girlfriend? Worried what she might say?"

Andy looked up to the stands where Enalyn was sitting. She wasn't looking in his direction.

"She's not my girlfriend," Andy mumbled.

Andy thought about the times Enalyn had told him about how Miriam Said had inspired her. He remembered how Enalyn bookmarked all the articles about Miriam Said — about how she'd come to Canada with her family from Egypt. About how she steadily rose up the swim rankings. Why shouldn't he let her know he was a fan?

"I'll do it," Andy said. "Just you watch."

11 MARK ON THE MARK

@MarkLi
You're going down, @TigerShark.

@TigerShark
@MarkLi dude do you really have to tweet at me? We're both here at provincials. Say it to my face.

@MarkLi
@TigerShark see you in the pool.

@Branko_Stimac
@TigerShark @MarkLi You two are the lamest twitterfighters in history.

@JoeXinEssex
@TigerShark @MarkLi @Branko_Stimac I've been following this twitterfight for weeks.

@ShelleyJ
@TigerShark @MarkLi @Branko_Stimac @JoeXinEssex
Me too. I think those two can't live without each other!

Finally it was time for the boys' 100-metre freestyle heats for 14-year-olds. Andy was in Heat 2. Ahead of him, getting ready for Heat 1, was Mark Li.

Andy stood on the deck as Mark got on the blocks. Mark saw Andy and drew his finger across his neck.

An announcer told the swimmers to get on their marks. Then the sound of the starting beep echoed off the walls.

The eight swimmers leapt off the blocks and hit the pool, swimming furiously. Li hit the wall at the other side two body-lengths ahead of the field. As Li turned, Andy didn't need to look at the clock to see that he was flying.

What the heck? thought Andy.

Li hit the wall to finish long before anyone else.

The clock read 54.95.

What? Andy thought. *He's never gone that fast!* I've *never gone that fast!*

The Eel walked up to Andy. "What the heck?"

"Shut up!" Andy said.

It was time for Heat 2 — and Andy was in lane 5. In a daze, he walked to the blocks. He kept replaying Mark Li's performance in his head. *Mark's strokes were perfect. His turns were sharp.* As Andy got ready to climb up onto the block, Coach Ocampo grabbed his shoulder.

"Andy, don't let Mark Li's swim get in your head. Nothing is won today. It's all won tomorrow. Your job is to swim a top-eight time right now, to get into tomorrow's final. Don't get out of your rhythm."

Andy looked up to the stands. His parents were still sitting far enough up to see the whole pool. But Enalyn was hanging over the rail that separated the bleachers from the pool deck. "Andy! Nail the entry! Turns out 56 isn't your number. But you can do this!"

Andy got up on the block. For the first time in a long time, the angle that let the swimmer lean over the pool felt strange. In the set position, with arms down and shoulders hunched, Andy felt like it would be easy to fall forward.

The starter — in a robotic voice that sounded like the evil robot from the *Galaxy Queen* cartoon — told the swimmers to get on their marks.

Andy waited.

Andy felt gravity pulling at him into the pool.

I can't get DQed, he thought. If he entered the water, he'd be disqualified. *I can't have come all this way to lose on a false start and get Dairy Queened.*

Then, the beep. And everything slowed down. Andy felt himself fall into the pool, nice and shallow. He surfaced clean, well into his strokes. His kicks were true. *One. Two. Three. Breathe.*

Through his goggles, Andy saw the black bar on the

pool's bottom that guided him in his lane. When the bar ended, he had to get ready to turn. He could tell by the lack of turbulence in his field of vision that he was in the lead.

He tucked his legs in tight and rotated in the water. He breathed out through his nose. He felt his feet brace against the wall as he pushed off hard to swim back the way he'd come. His internal clock was telling him that this was the fastest he'd ever gone.

One. Two. Three.

Again.

The black line in the pool was coming to an end. Andy was nearing the finish. Two, three more powerful strokes. A pair of thrusting kicks. He stretched, fingertips touching the wall.

He'd won the heat!

And then he looked up at the clock.

55.45.

It was his best time ever. But it was a half-second slower than what Mark Li had posted in his heat.

Andy heard Enalyn screaming. "You see! Look at that! Better than 56!"

But, at the moment, Andy felt like the slowest racer in the world. He wondered if this was how Zach felt.

★★★

Andy had put on his warm-up suit and was sitting in the stands. He'd just finished swimming the anchor leg for

COBRA's relay team. He had made up half a lap on the field, but he couldn't make up the deficit. COBRA was a small team, and the other swimmers simply couldn't keep pace with the other teams. COBRA didn't qualify for the next day's final.

Now Andy had just one event to focus on, the 100-metre freestyle final.

Coach Ocampo sat down next to him.

"You seem awfully worried," said the coach.

"Shouldn't I be?" said Andy. "Mark Li has been at least a half-second slower than me at every meet this year. And now he posts a crazy time."

"A crazy time in the *preliminary* heats," Coach Ocampo said. "Really, all he did was swim a fast qualifying time."

"And?"

"And, if you spend the rest of the day worried about Mark Li, you won't be going as fast as you can tomorrow. Worry about what *you* can do. Go to the warm-up pool. Work on some entries. Work on your rhythm. Worry about going as fast as you can. Mark Li is going to do whatever he's going to do. You can't control that. What you have to focus on is getting faster, saving your best for the final and then executing."

"He's right, you know," said Enalyn, sitting down on the other side of Andy. "Just pretend you're swimming in that lane at Earnscliffe. That you're by yourself. Just you and the clock."

"Yeah, I guess you're right."

"Now, let's get your mind off tomorrow's final," said Enalyn with a smile. "Miriam Said's heat is coming up."

The dare! Andy thought. He'd become so distracted by Mark Li's time that he'd almost forgotten about the dare.

Enalyn took Andy by the hand. She led him to a couple of seats that offered a decent view of the pool through the crowd of people gathered to watch the first heat of the women's 100-metre breaststroke. Miriam Said's orange cap was like a beacon. She waited for all the competitors to take their marks before finally discarding her long robe and getting onto the blocks in lane 4.

The gun sounded, and she was in the water. Her head popped up and she took a mighty breath. She brought her hands together as if she were praying, then drove them apart, with each movement thrusting herself forward.

By the wall, Miriam Said was already body-lengths ahead of the field. When she turned, she had the pool to herself in front of her. The other seven swimmers were still going in the other direction.

By the time the rest of the field had finished their turns, Miriam Said was ahead by a third of the pool. She smoothly coasted to the finish.

Andy knew it was time to dash out of his chair, run across the deck and give Miriam Said a kiss. His brain told him to get up, but his body remained rooted to the chair.

"Did you see that?" Enalyn cried. "She's so good!"

Enalyn clapped and clapped and clapped. She didn't notice two swimmers walking right up to where she and Andy sat and looking Andy in the eye.

It was the pair of swimmers from Leslieville.

"What the hell?" said the first one.

"Tomorrow. After the final. I promise," Andy said.

"Okay. But that's your last chance," said the second swimmer. They shot Enalyn admiring glances as they walked away.

Enalyn turned to Andy. "What the hell was that? Who are those guys?"

"It's nothing," said Andy. "They're just some guys who were bugging me earlier today. Really, it's nothing at all."

12 MAKING IT

Andy's arms were covered in red patches.

After the first day of racing was over, he hadn't joined his parents at the Super 8 where Coach Ocampo had booked rooms for the team and some of the parents. Instead, Andy got into the warm-up pool, then got out. He plunged off the blocks. He did it again. And again. When his entry was perfect, there was no sting on the skin of his arms. But, when he missed his angle, even by a bit, there was a smacking sensation when he hit the water. And with every bad entry, the stings added up. By the second day of the meet, as the clock ticked down to the 100-metre final, Andy's arms looked like they had broken out into a rash.

The starter announced that it was time for the boys to get up on the blocks. Mark Li was in lane 3. Andy was in lane 4.

"Four is a very unlucky number in Chinese," Mark told Andy, who stood on the block next to him. "I just wanted to point that out."

Andy closed his eyes. *Entry has to be perfect. One. Two. Three. Breathe.* "Nice of you to finally talk to me, Mark," he said. "Or do you want to find your phone so you can tweet that? We can race without you."

He opened his eyes. He looked through his grey, frosted goggles toward the lane in front of him. He could see the packed stands in the reflection of the still water.

"I saved my best for this meet," Andy heard Li say.

Andy didn't take his eyes off the lane. "I saved my best for this meet, too," he said.

They were interrupted by the robotic voice of the race official. "Gentlemen, take your marks."

Andy took a deep breath. He had to time it perfectly. As soon as he heard the beep, he needed to move. His entry had to be smooth. He couldn't afford even a fraction of a second's hesitation on the blocks.

Then, a splash. Someone was in the water!

False start! thought Andy. The swimmer in lane 7 had plunged into the water before the beep sounded.

Dairy Queened! The race was done for the swimmer in lane 7.

The swimmers were told to reset.

Andy imagined he was a tiger shark, gliding through the water, chasing his prey.

The boys were once again told to take their marks.

Once again, Andy looked into the water ahead of him. It was still rippling slightly from the false start a minute before.

Focus on the beep, Andy thought.

And then it came. Andy reacted. He hit the water. His entry was clean, leaving only a tiny little splash behind.

Andy pushed forward under the water, reaching ahead to maximize his distance. He broke the surface and his right arm rotated into a stroke. Then the left. Each hand glided through the water. Each thumb pointed down, acting like a fin when a hand hit the water. His kicking was in rhythm. And he pushed hard, but not so hard that he came out of his cadence. He made sure to keep his strokes true and concentrated on completing the cycles faster.

He got to the wall. His internal clock was telling him that he was going even faster than he'd swum the day before. Faster than he'd ever gone.

It was time for the turn. As Andy got close to the end of the lane, he took a breath and dove down into the water, somersaulting and twisting at the same time. He pushed off the wall. His feet felt like they had springs in them. And then he was off, back to the start.

One. Two. Three. Breathe.

Andy kept thinking about his rhythm, making sure all his limbs were working in concert with each other. Each kick of his legs helped maximize his speed. Each stroke was true.

The finishing pad was ten metres away. Nine. Eight. Seven. Six. Five. Four. Three . . .

Andy stretched forward, trying to tap his fingers on the pad as quickly as he could.

Contact.

Andy sprung out of the water, ripping off his goggles in one mighty swipe. He noticed Mark Li was looking up at the clock. Which one had made it to the wall first?

There was a wait of a few seconds, then the times flashed.

Mark Li had gone even faster than he had in the preliminary heat. His time was 54.89.

But Andy's time was 54.78. By a tenth of a second, Andy had won!

Andy thrust his arms into the air. He got out of the pool, put on the towel Coach Ocampo held out for him, then jumped into the air.

"Whoa, don't break those ankles!" came a voice from behind Andy.

It was Travis Holloway. Andy spun and shook the coach's hand.

"I heard you were okay at surfing on a flutterboard," said Holloway. "Now I see why they call you Tiger Shark."

"Sir, I m-m-mean, it's an honour . . ." Andy stuttered.

"Honour? Well, son, you're going to be seeing a lot of me. I'm going to watch you race at nationals. Ready for the trip to Edmonton?"

Andy could feel his face being stretched by his wide

smile. His dad was in the stands, arms in the air. His mom's tears had smudged her mascara. And Enalyn blew him a kiss.

Enalyn blew him a kiss? *Wait!* thought Andy. *Did Enalyn really just do that?*

@TigerShark
@MarkLi Mark, you swam a great time. It just wasn't quite as fast as ME.

@TigerShark
@MarkLi Oh Mark, Mark, you there? What, you aren't on Twitter?

@TigerShark
@MarkLi Are you kidding me? Did you really block me?

Twitter
The user @MarkLi does not exist.

Andy put down his phone and looked at Enalyn, who sat in the stands next to him.

"I think Mark Li just deleted his Twitter account," he said.

"Oh, so sad," laughed Enalyn. "Are you going to miss your Twitter friend?"

"Very funny."

Since he had his phone in hand, Andy checked his

Twitter stats. He had sent out a tweet link to the YouTube video Swim Ontario had posted of the 100-metre final. It had been shared only twice. He then surfed to the YouTube video of him surfing across Earnscliffe Pool. It had more than five million hits.

Andy's father walked to where Andy and Enalyn were sitting, a soft drink in his hand. He sat down next to Andy.

Andy showed him the screen. "Look at this, Dad. I set the fastest time in Ontario, and a couple of people watched that. I surfed, and, well, *a lot* of people watched that."

"Oh, András, you will understand this one day," his father said. "If you do something excellent, *some* people will notice. But if you do something silly, *everybody* notices."

"And, Andy, you only set that time a couple of hours ago," Enalyn said. "Give it time."

"But when the flutterboard video went out, it was shared hundreds of times within hours," said Andy.

Enalyn shrugged.

"András, some people watched you surf across the pool. Sure, pretty cool. But what did that give you?"

"I got a lot of followers on Twitter."

"And what does that mean?"

"It means, more people check to see what I have to say or post when I update my Twitter account."

"Okay, Andy, I will pretend that you just spoke

English there. So, does this mean you have many new friends?"

"No, just thousands of new followers."

"Followers? And you lead them . . . where?"

Andy laughed. "No, Dad. I don't lead them anywhere. They just check in to see what I do."

"Sounds like communism," his father said. "It's best if other people don't know what you do."

"Why?"

"Because if people know what you do all the time, you're not free. You can't be your own person. This Twitter sounds like Big Brother watching you."

"It's just other people."

"Oh, so the mob watches you. So much *better*."

His dad took a long draw from his pop, making a long sucking, gurgling sound. He finished it off with a loud "ahhhh."

"Well, when are you going to leave, you two?" his father asked. "Your mother and I are about to drive back to Brampton. You could come back with us. You have no more races left, right? We can go celebrate at home."

"No, Dad, I think I'll take the van back with Coach Ocampo," said Andy. "I'd still like to see a few more races. And it looks bad if a provincial champ leaves the event when there's other swimmers still left to race."

Especially Miriam Said, Andy thought.

"Okay, okay, I'm going to go track down your

mom," his dad said. Before he turned to leave, Andy's father put his hand on his son's shoulder. "I'm proud of you. You were flying in that pool. All those hours, working with your coach, they paid off. And you could also go change. You're still lounging around in your swim suit!"

13 THE DARE

Andy and Enalyn watched race after race.

"Miriam's race is coming up next," she said.

"How come you don't go up and talk to her?" Andy asked. "I mean, she's been in the building for the last couple of days."

"Oh, come on," she said. "She tweeted me once and I was, like, floored. I don't need to go up to her and bother her. I'm just a spectator here."

"Well, I'm going to go down and watch the race from the deck," Andy said, and got up.

"What? You're leaving?" Enalyn coughed. "We've got a great view from these seats. We can see the whole pool."

"Um, I need to say hi to someone on the deck," Andy said.

"Now?"

"Um, yeah."

"Well, Andy, I'm going to stay here. Sometimes you act so weird. Are you sure you're not a superhero with a secret identity or something? That would explain you getting up and leaving right before the race."

Andy shrugged. He walked down off the stands and onto the deck. In the competition pool, Miriam Said was getting on the lane-5 block for her signature event, the 100-metre breaststroke.

The beep sounded, Said plunged into the pool. She surfaced well ahead of the pack. With each stroke, her orange swim cap would submerge, then rise back up. She made a whistling sound when she exhaled. The race wasn't even close. She got to the halfway mark well ahead of the field. She shot through the water. On the deck, dozens of people were holding up their phones, taking videos of the race.

Miriam Said hit the finishing pad. People on deck whooped and cheered. She waved to them as the other racers finally got to the end. Andy pushed through the bodies so he could get closer to the far end of the pool. With a provincial medal around his neck, no one questioned him.

This was his chance. Miriam Said had just gotten out of the pool.

Andy knew what he had to do. *Rookie has to finish the initiation, right?* he thought to himself as he dashed forward. The sound of his flip-flops smacked off the deck like dozens of slaps.

No one tried to stop him. He stood in front of Miriam Said. The words came out of his mouth like someone else was saying them. It felt like he was out of his body, watching another person take over his speech and actions.

"What a great race!" he said. "And you, really, are like, wow. I just wanted to say that."

"Um, thanks?" Miriam Said raised an eyebrow.

"I'm Andy. I'll see you at nationals."

I've done it, Andy thought. *I talked to her.*

And then, Andy hugged Miriam Said. He whispered "congratulations" in her ear, and then delivered a small peck to her cheek. His towel had slipped off his shoulders, and for a second, he could feel her wet skin against his. As he turned and walked away, he knew that the people on the deck were staring at him. He saw that some had their phones pointed directly at him. But he didn't care.

When he got back up the stairs to where Enalyn was sitting, she was staring at him with wide eyes. Her hand was over her mouth. Through her fingers, she whispered, "Andy. What. Have. You. Done?"

"I talked to Miriam Said. Like I said I would."

"No, Andy! You didn't just talk to her! You hugged her and then you kissed her! Before she could get her robe back on!"

"I just said something into her ear!"

"Stop lying, Andy, I could see it. It was a kiss! And you were both practically naked! Get away from me! I don't want to talk to you right now!"

Stunned, Andy headed for the men's change room. The two Leslieville swimmers were there.

"Did you see it? I did it," Andy said.

"I can't believe it. You should never have done that. Miriam Said is like, awesome."

The second Leslieville swimmer nodded. "Dude, we can't even talk to you anymore. You'd better get out of here. You're gonna be in so much crap. I mean, it's bad enough to kiss any competitor, but Miriam Said? We all respect her beliefs."

What? Andy's jaw dropped. He watched as the two swimmers packed their bags as quickly as they could.

"What do you mean, her beliefs?"

"Dude," said the first Leslieville swimmer. "Don't you know anything? Her family is Muslim. She petitioned Swim Canada to let her wear a swimsuit that covered her arms and legs — and her head."

"Wait, yeah, I kind of remember hearing that," Andy said. Enalyn was always going on about her idol. "But they said no."

"Still, dude, you've got to know that she's not cool with anyone she doesn't know touching her. Especially when she's not covered up."

"Sorry, we can't be around you, Tiger Shark!" the second Leslieville swimmer said as he rushed out the door. "No way are they gonna let you race at nationals!"

It was like Andy was glued to the spot on the change-room bench. A minute after the two swimmers left, someone else entered. It was Travis Holloway. His face was red.

"So, here you are," he said to Andy. He crouched down so he could look the young swimmer in the eye. And, even though they were close to each other, Holloway spoke as loudly as he could.

"What was the meaning of that? Were you trying to embarrass our country's finest swimmer? Or yourself? What? What!"

Andy realized he'd made a horrible mistake.

"Coach," he said quietly. "It was a stunt. Someone dared me to . . ."

"I don't care!" the coach roared. "I don't care who put you up to it, or who dared you to do it. The fact is, *you did it*!"

"But, Coach, can't we just forget it happened?"

"You just don't get it, do you?" Holloway said. "You of all people! You're the kid who became the Internet star! Did you see all the people who caught that on their phones? They got you on video, don't you get it?"

Andy didn't say a word. As Travis Holloway stormed out, Andy tiptoed to his locker, opened the door and dug out his phone.

On Twitter, it was already making the rounds. There was already a vine that was being shared and shared some more.

CHECK OUT THIS VINE OF CANADIAN CHAMP @TheREALMiriamSaid being attacked!

Attacked? Andy thought.

Andy clicked on the vine. It showed Miriam Said smiling. And then, there was Andy. The camera closed in, so all the viewer could see was Andy and Miriam from the shoulders up. Andy watched himself draw close and deliver a kiss. He watched as his towel slipped down and his bare shoulders brushed Miriam's.

And he saw Miriam Said's eyes open wide as she pulled away. After Andy had fled, Miriam Said's hand went over her mouth. An official came over and tried to console her.

Andy recognized Miriam Said's actions. She felt like she had been attacked. By Andy.

14 UNPLUGGING

@MaryMillions

Check this out: @TheREALMiriamSaid attacked at provincials! Video link: www.youtube.com/watch?v=SuRzUDIlAXz

@RealSwimFan2016

@MaryMillions So, who is that with @TheREALMiriamSaid! Did he just run up naked and kiss her????

@Women4Equality

Have you seen this video? A female athlete shamed! www.youtube.com/watch?v=SuRzUDIlAXz

Retweeted 287 times.

@SportsShorts

Canadian Olympic hopeful @TheREALMiriamSaid and an unwelcome fan.

@CanadaNewsUpdate
Champion Said target of sexist Islamophobic act.

@CanadaEh
Confirming that the idiot in that video is @TigerShark time for @SwimCanada to do the right thing. BAN HIM.

@SportsNutz
@TheREALMiriamSaid is Muslim. Not a REAL Canadian! She shouldn't even be allowed in the stands! Yay @TigerShark.

@KristenKrezowski
@SportsNutz @TigerShark yer both pathetic. Shame on you.

@ReplaySports
See the video everyone is talking about! ONT swim champ @TheREALMiriamSaid assaulted by @TigerShark!

"Assaulted?" Andy said as he flicked his thumb up and down on his screen. "I didn't assault anyone! It was a hug and a peck!"

Enalyn sat in the front of the van with Coach Ocampo. Neither had said a word to Andy since they pulled out of the parking lot at McMaster. They were on Highway 403, headed back toward Brampton. Andy sat in the back of the van with the Eel.

"I am sure it'll blow over," the Eel said. "I mean, it's totally obvious that you didn't attack her. But it does look kinda creepy."

"I don't know what this is about," Andy sighed. "I mean, I didn't really know what I was doing. It was a dare! It was innocent. I hope this isn't going to be awkward when I see her at nationals."

Andy heard Enalyn make a harrumphing sound in the front seat.

@CalgaryWomensCentre
Shocking video. @TigerShark should be ashamed.

@CanadaSportsChannel
From Internet hero to zero. @TigerShark outed as misogynist and racist.

@CatherineBHorvath
Sign the Change.org petition. Ban @TigerShark from @SwimCanada for life!

Andy clicked on the link that took him to the Change.org petition.

> Given that sport should reflect our values, and be inclusive, we feel that Swim Canada must not allow @TigerShark, Andy Kovacs of COBRA swim club, to swim in any events or represent our national swim

program in any way. His actions against Miriam Said show a blatant disregard for the rights of women and people of all faiths. Our national teams should represent the values of Canadian diversity. We, the undersigned, demand that Andy Kovacs not be allowed to compete at another provincial competition or any national meet.

Andy swallowed hard when he saw that the petition had already been signed 676 times. He refreshed the page; 684 times. Again; 688.

"How did they know it was me?" Andy asked the Eel. "I mean, this only happened a couple of hours ago."

The Eel laughed. "Andy, dude, you're an Internet star! How many hits did that flutterboard thing get? Someone got a video of you today and posted it right away. Really, I'm surprised it took that long for someone to put two and two together. It's all over the Internet that the flutterboard guy is the same as the Miriam Said Bandit."

"Wait, did you just give me a nickname?"

"Dude, this will make you a rock star in the end, just you watch!"

★★★

Andy couldn't sleep. His mom had made paprika chicken and dumplings, his favourite dish, to celebrate his win at provincials. Luckily, his mom and dad didn't know anything about Andy's latest claim to social media fame.

Andy asked to be excused and went to his room.

"Nothing's wrong," he told his parents. "After everything that's happened today, I'm exhausted."

"No worries, son," his dad said. "Sleep in. You've earned it."

But Andy didn't sleep. He couldn't sleep. After climbing a steep set of stairs to get to his room, he turned his phone back on.

@Freddie2000
Hey @TigerShark, go kill yourself.

@LockedDown77
@TigerShark yer a ladies man what a player ha.

@StaceyByrnes3809
@TigerShark You make me vomit. The way you touched her was disgusting.

All of the tweets aimed at him were like this. There were thousands of them.

Andy decided to delete his Twitter account.

When Andy saw there were more than 2,000 notifications on his Facebook account, he deleted that, too.

His Gmail inbox had hundreds of unread messages.

Instead of reading them, he turned off his phone.

He couldn't take it anymore.

Andy pulled the curtains to shut out the streetlight that shone right into his room. He lay on his bed. He felt drained. But he couldn't sleep. He stared at the red light from the smoke detector on the ceiling. He tried to remember every move he had made before hugging Miriam Said. It was all a blur. Surely, in a day or so, everyone would forget, right?

Finally, there was a loud knock on the door.

"Yes?"

"András, it's me. Mom. We just got a strange phone call downstairs. It's almost midnight but there was a Travis Holloway on the line. From Swim Canada."

"What?"

"He just wanted me to give you a message. He wants to talk via Skype tomorrow morning. At nine. He has your handle, whatever that means, he says. Just accept his, um, contact request, that's it. He says it's urgent."

***

Andy sat on his bed. It was 8:55 a.m. and he had just activated the Skype app on his phone. The screen went blue as the system automatically logged him on. Once he got to his contacts screen, he accepted the invitation from TravisHollowaySWIM.

He waited five minutes. Then ten. Then half an hour.

His dad knocked at the door. "So, have you heard from this coach yet? They probably want to fly you to Edmonton first class!"

"Not yet," Andy said. He looked at the alarm clock on his night table. It read 9:32 a.m.

And then the icon on the screen started to vibrate. The Skype screen showed an incoming call from TravisHollowaySWIM. Andy hit the video-chat button. He saw a pixelated blur of two silhouettes that suddenly came into focus. Travis Holloway was sitting next to a woman with grey hair and dark, heavy eyebrows that sat angrily over her wire spectacles.

Travis spoke. "Andy, sorry to keep you waiting. But our meeting went over time. The meeting was about you. This is Marguerite D'Youville, the president of Swim Canada. We've spent much of last night and this morning discussing what happened. We also spoke with Miriam."

"But . . ." Andy began. "I thought this was going to be about nationals."

"Andy, zip it. It's better for you the less you talk," said Holloway. "Unfortunately, this talk *is* about nationals. We came to a decision that we can't allow you to swim at them. In about two hours, Swim Canada is going to issue a press release announcing that you've been banned from competing. And the length of the ban is indefinite. That means there is no planned date to reinstate you."

Andy felt the tears start up in his eyes. "Seriously?"

The president said nothing. She just looked forward at the screen as Holloway kept talking.

"Look, kid," Holloway's voice softened. "You screwed up. Even if I believe that you didn't know how offended Miriam would be by your actions, you should have known better. You say you were put up to this by some other kids. Well, we asked around all the swim teams last night, and no one says they dared you to do this. Really, I have no doubt that someone *did* put you up to this, but there's no way to prove it. And it doesn't change the fact that you could have said no.

"On Facebook and Twitter, everyone is talking about swimming today," he continued, "but it's not about racing. It's about this. The sponsors who pay the bills for nationals want you gone. Women's groups want you gone. Islamic groups want you gone. Heck, I need to tell you that I've gotten a few calls from government MPs who want you gone."

"B-b-but I wanted to be like you, I wanted to go to the Olympics . . ." Andy protested.

Finally, the president spoke. "So, you think you can go to the Olympics? You don't have the class to be an Olympian!"

She got up, smoothed her long black skirt and left the room, leaving Holloway alone.

"Look, kid, keep your head down. Don't talk

to anyone. And please take down that embarrassing fundraising site you created."

The next thing Andy heard was a click, and he saw a CALL ENDED message appear on the screen.

15 FOUND OUT

Andy was still trying to dry his tears when his mom opened the door to his room. She didn't knock.

"Come downstairs. Now," she said coldly.

"But, Mom, I just got some bad news . . ."

"NOW, young man."

Shaking, he rose from his chair and followed his mom down past the kitchen to the living room. His dad sat on the couch, watching the end of the Sports Channel's *Misplays of the Week*.

"Congratulations. You were number one on this week's list of misplays," said Andy's dad. "So when were you planning to tell us about this?"

"Dad, Mom, I'm so sorry," Andy blubbered. "It was a dare. I mean . . ." *What else could go wrong?*

"Well, after seeing your antics on TV, I thought, *That couldn't be my son*," said Andy's mom. "I thought about how you're always trying to do the right thing. The only person who has said a bad thing about you is that math teacher of yours. And then, I thought to myself, *Funny, it's July, and I haven't seen Andy's report card yet.*"

Oh no.

"So, András, I logged in. It said that the reminders were e-mailed out weeks ago. Funny how we didn't get them. Then, I saw your math mark: a 51."

"Well, Mr. Chalmers is an awfully tough marker," said Andy.

"Andy, listen to yourself!" his father roared. Andy hadn't heard his dad raise his voice like that in a long, long time. "You nearly flunked the course, and you're blaming the teacher. This is math. It's either right or wrong. A teacher can't be a hard marker when it comes to math. You might have passed by the skin of your teeth, but your mark is about as D-minus as a D-minus can be!"

"And then," said his dad, "we did a little more digging into our so famous son. We saw the fundraising page that you created."

"I'm just about to delete that," Andy said.

"Don't you think you should have said something to us?" Andy could see his dad was shaking as he said this. "Do you know how embarrassing it is for us? To have our son asking for money from strangers? To have him begging so publicly? The deal was you'd raise some cash through work, and we'd come up with the rest."

"But, Dad, you're not working . . ."

"For now! Just for now! András, this wasn't about

you trying to help us! This was about going on the Internet with another reason to say, 'hey, look at me!' Well, guess what? People are looking at you!"

"I knew it was a mistake for you to have school, a part-time job and the swim team at the same time," said his mom.

"Mom, Dad." Andy started to cry again. "You don't have to worry about the swimming anymore. They're not going to let me swim at nationals."

Andy's dad softened his voice. "Well, it looks like you've messed up school and swimming."

It's a good thing I still have the comic-book store, thought Andy. "Well, I should go. I need to be at the mall at noon."

***

"Andy, wait! Come here. I need to talk to you!" Mr. Patel called out as Andy walked past the new-release rack.

"I know what you did," he said. "I've got hundreds of e-mails and Facebook messages about you this morning."

"You did? Why?"

"On our store's Facebook page, you were listed as a staff member. The Internet mob found you. People are already talking about boycotting the shop! They're tweeting to all the comic publishers that they should take us off their distribution lists! Look!"

Andy went behind the counter to look at the store laptop. It was logged in to Comic Relief's Facebook page.

Mary MacDonnell
I CANNOT believe that you have that sexist jerk working at your store. NEVER SHOPPING THERE.

Harvey Visscher
I can't support a shop that supports racism.

Danisha Danisha
+1 Shame

It went on and on.

"What are we going to do?" Andy asked.

"I'm sorry, Andy." Mr. Patel winced. "There is no *we*. The question is, what am *I* going to do? I'm going to have to let you go. And that's not all. I'm going to have to ban you from the store. I have to save my business."

"This isn't fair! It was meant to be a prank!" Andy cried.

"Andy, this isn't about if you're a good kid or a bad kid or a kid who made a stupid mistake. They are out for blood. And if I don't cut my ties with you, the store could die."

Mr. Patel leaned down and reached under the counter. He pulled out a large envelope with ANDY KOVACS written on it.

"Termination papers," said Mr. Patel.

Andy accepted the envelope. He opened it and saw a blank line that was highlighted.

"Sign there," said Mr. Patel, handing Andy a pen.

Andy signed.

"Now, Andy, I have to ask you to go," said Mr. Patel. "I'm just about to post that you're no longer an employee and have been banned. I'm sorry it had to end up like this."

★★★

After two days of staying in the house, Andy was about to go crazy. His parents agreed that he could go to Earnscliffe Pool — but only because Coach Ocampo had called.

"He said he absolutely needed to see you," his mom said.

Andy put his swim gear in his bag. He hadn't been in the water since Hamilton.

"You come right home after you meet the coach," said his mother.

"Mom, that's the second time you've said it. I will, I will."

"And stay off your phone."

"Mom, I deleted all my accounts. My phone is just a phone now. But can I ask how long am I going to be grounded for?"

His mom scrunched up her face; a line of wrinkles appeared on her forehead. "Oh, András. You think this is a grounding? What we're trying to do is protect you! Look, we have received some pretty scary e-mails. There are people who tell us that they're going to find you and hurt you. So once you get on the bike, you don't stop. Just go up the street to the pool."

"People are sending us threats?"

"András, don't worry about it. We just need to wait until the next Internet sensation and everyone out there forgets about you."

"But, Mom, what I did . . . I mean, I didn't mean any harm."

"András, it used to be that if you did something bad, you could make up for it. You could say sorry. Even criminals, well, they go to jail for what they do and then they get let out. But now, it just snowballs. People aren't happy unless they bury you. They get their pounds of flesh, and they want more! More! They want to kick you when you're down. So take your bike. Go out through the backyard and cut across the playground. Head through the parks, not the main streets."

"Okay."

Andy did as he was told, rolling through the courtyard's playground and across to the back end of the

Darras Court townhouse complex. He took an access path to the park that didn't take him close to the main street. He rode through a series of greenbelts to the rec centre.

As he entered the building, he was greeted by the smell of fries and doughnuts from the concession stand. There was a showcase filled with trophies from previous COBRA swim teams.

Andy walked toward the COBRA office and knocked on the door.

"Coach?"

He opened the door and saw Coach Ocampo sitting at his desk.

"So, Andy, why did you do it?" he asked as Andy sat down across from him.

"I screwed up. A couple of other swimmers dared me to do it. I didn't think it'd become a big thing."

"Well, no matter who dared you to do what, Andy, it *has* become a big thing. A real big thing." Coach Ocampo turned his computer screen so Andy could see it. "This here is our Facebook page. Look at some of the posts."

Lundmark

Don't ever let that jerk swim for your crap club ever again!

Melanie Yaremchuk
I was thinking about enrolling my son in your program. But I won't, now. What do you teach those kids?

Jason The Jason
Someone needs to smack that Andy kid hard.

Nola Jenkinson
Everyone. Please follow this change.org link. These are a list of Brampton businesses that sponsor the swim club. Let's let these businesses know that if Andy Kovacs, the "Tiger Shark," continues to swim for COBRA, we won't support them. Boycott!

Andy saw that the link had been shared 598 times.

"I could keep scrolling down, but I won't," said Coach Ocampo. "Look, I understand you didn't mean to screw up. But we need the money from our sponsors. The local bank branch. The coffee shop. That restaurant down the street. And they're all up in arms about this. A couple of sponsors have told me that if the club keeps you, they're out. No more money."

"Because of me."

"Not because of you, but because of what you *did*."

"Coach, are you telling me I can't swim for COBRA anymore?"

"I'm really sorry, Andy. I wish there was another way. You're the best swimmer I've ever coached. But

I have to put the needs of the club first. And the club needs its sponsors."

Andy rose from his chair. "Well, Coach, then write a Facebook post that I'm no longer with the team. You should also tweet it out. Make a sign and put it on the door of the rec centre. But please, do me one favour. Tell them I quit. Tell them that for the good of the club, I decided I wasn't going to swim anymore. Tell them that they've won."

16 ALONE IN THE LANE

www.MiriamSaid.blogspot.ca

I have just been informed that TIGER SHARK has quit his swim club.

To most of my followers, I know this must feel like justice has been served. But to me, I'm not sure.

I want to make this clear: the swimmer Andy Kovacs has not contacted me since the incident. He has not apologized for his actions. But I find that all of the attention paid to this incident is an unnecessary distraction.

Swimming changed my life. I come from a family of Egyptian immigrants — and swimming gave me a chance to express myself. It gave me a chance to learn about myself. It allowed me to feel confident. I can't imagine where my life would have gone if that was taken away from me.

As some of you know, last year I applied to Swim Canada to see if I could get an exception to the rule that doesn't allow for swimsuits that cover the arms and legs. That was unsuccessful, because the ruling was that such a suit would give me a competitive advantage.

While I remain dedicated to my faith, I made the decision to keep swimming. Without a swim hijab, and in a regulation suit. But I try to be as humble, as modest as possible.

So I feel that what Andy Kovacs did to me was inappropriate and wrong. But knowing that he's quit his swim team also feels wrong. Why? I have uncles and aunts who were involved in the Arab Spring back in Cairo. They protested because we should all have freedom of expression. They protested because they didn't want to live in a place where people could be punished over and over and over again. I feel that if I condemn Andy Kovacs for his actions, I'll be betraying those ideals. I think he has suffered enough for what he's done wrong. That's all I wanted to say.

COMMENTS

SaidFan4Life

Miriam! What he did to you was horrible! He should never swim again!

Flipper23
Noooooo!!! It's not wrong that he's banned! You gotta stand up! Too many women deal with this kinda CRAP! Be STRONG!

WaterOnTheBrain
Miss Said, it's not your fault. He did what he did, and he's being punished for it. It's not enough, if you ask me. He should have been charged!

DragonBoat
We can't forget, why should we forgive!

★★★

The sun had set, but the sky wasn't completely dark. There were traces of orange and dark blue as Andy locked up his bike and walked into the rec centre.

The sign on the door said that the pool would close at 11:00 p.m. Andy looked at his watch. It was 9:45. The pool would be close to empty.

He walked into an empty change room and breathed a sigh of relief. He changed into his swim shorts, showered and opened up the door to the pool deck just a crack. He could see that there was one other swimmer in the pool — an old guy in the slow lane.

Andy pushed open the door wide and walked toward the pool.

"Well, look what the cat dragged in," came a voice from high atop the lifeguard's chair.

Andy turned. "Um, hi, Enalyn."

"Bet you were hoping not to see me."

"I called ahead and they said you weren't gonna be working tonight."

"Ha, someone called in sick and I got the shift."

"I just wanted to swim in peace. I haven't been in the pool for weeks."

"From what I've seen said about you on Twitter, I'm surprised you can go out at all."

"I'm taking a break from everything. Twitter. Facebook. My mom and dad are going through my e-mail before they let me see it. I had to beg and beg them to let me come here tonight."

"So tell me why I should be talking to you, Andy. I was really mad at you for dragging me into this mess. I am still getting a few tweets a day about how terrible it must be to be the Tiger Shark's girlfriend."

Girlfriend? thought Andy.

"You're thinking, what does she mean by *girlfriend*? Well, all it took was someone to post that they saw me cheering you on at provincials, and I've been taking some real grief."

"Sorry."

"I'm almost over it. I'm collateral damage. I get it. But you still shoulda called me to apologize. Again."

"But after the meet, the van, you didn't want to talk to me."

"And for good reason! You really pissed me off with that stunt! But you think just wallowing away in your pool of self-pity, without telling the people around you that you're sorry, that's better? Huh?"

Andy stood quietly on the deck. The senior splashed by on the outside lane, either deaf or ignoring the dressing-down Andy was getting.

"Um, Andy," said Enalyn, putting a finger to her chin. "This is the part where you say, 'Sorry, you're right Enalyn.' And, 'Once again, please forgive me, Enalyn.' And, once we get past that, we can get to, 'Is there any way you can help me, Enalyn?'"

Andy tapped his foot on the deck. He tapped it some more. He looked at his feet until it struck him how ugly and misshaped his big toes were. *Why haven't I noticed that before?*

Finally, he exhaled, hard — as if he'd just finished a 100-metre front crawl in less than 55 seconds. "Okay, Enalyn, the reason I didn't call was because I was embarrassed. And, since I'm apologizing, I should also mention you were right about the math thing, too. I got a 51. That's a big topic of discussion in the Kovacs household. And so, I'm sorry."

Enalyn climbed down from the chair, then walked over to Andy.

"Andy, get in the pool. Clear your head. And maybe I'll think a bit on something that can help you."

"You don't think I'm a racist sexist pig that deserves

to never swim again or have a job or have a life?"

"Well, you may be the most clueless guy in the world, but I know you're not a racist. The jury is out on the sexist pig thing, after that performance you gave. Mostly, I don't believe anyone deserves to be punished forever."

Andy walked to the far lane and plunged into the water. The cool blast of water gave him goosebumps. It made him feel like weeks of dirt was being washed from his body. He glided forward, kicking softly. He wasn't trying to go fast; he just needed to be back in the water. He wasn't Tiger Shark anymore. He felt like a leaf floating on the water.

Back and forth he went. He remembered the joy of feeling as light as a feather in the water. He dove deep so he could touch the bottom of the pool with his outstretched fingertips.

And then he heard a voice.

"Andy!" said Enalyn. "It's almost eleven. Pool's closing!"

He'd been in the water for a little more than an hour, but it had only felt like a couple of minutes.

He hauled himself out of the pool. The old guy had left. It was just Andy and Enalyn.

"I wish you didn't have to close the pool," said Andy. "That's the best I've felt in weeks."

"But, Andy, you weren't trying to go that fast or anything," said Enalyn. "It wasn't very Tiger Shark–like. You were . . ."

"Enjoying myself. I guess I forgot just how much I like to be in the water."

"I'm doing the late shift again tomorrow," said Enalyn. "It's never busy, so you should come back again."

***

And Andy did come back. The next night, he got to the pool and dove in. He splashed and flipped. He tried to see how long he could hold his breath. And, finally, he got out, tossed a flutterboard into the pool and then made a run for the rope. He swung out and landed. But he hit the flutterboard all wrong. The board shot up in the air as Andy flopped into the water.

Enalyn laughed. "Oh, I wish I'd had my camera on! Tiger Shark flutterboard surfing, part two!"

Then Andy did something he hadn't done in weeks. He laughed. And laughed. He laughed so hard that he started to cough.

"I think I've got to come out of the pool now." He forced the words through a series of hacks.

Enalyn came down from her chair and sat across from Andy, with just her feet in the water.

"Andy, I've got an idea. For you. To help you. It might work, it might not. But I'm not sure if I should tell you, considering your past history . . ."

"Of making bad decisions and ignoring your advice?"

"Well look at the *new* Andy! This new self-awareness suits you. Too bad it took you having to do the dumbest thing in the world to take a hard look at yourself."

"Over the last few weeks, I've spent a lot of time alone. In my room. Reading old comics. Listening to music. No Internet."

"Well, I could be a lousy friend and tell you it's all going to be okay, but that would be a lie. But I do have an idea that might help you pull out of this dive. I have to tell you, though. It'll require you to do the thing that you don't want to do the most."

"And what's that?"

"You have to go back on social media."

"Oh no." Andy shook his head. "No way. No!"

"Okay, forget about it then." Enalyn got up. "Gotta close the pool, Andy."

Andy headed for the change room. He remembered what it was like to be in there with the Eel and the rest of his COBRA teammates. Even Zach. The jokes. The laughs. Now all he heard was a loud, ringing echo when he closed a locker door.

He headed outside to the bike rack. Enalyn's bike was next to his. He waited for her to come out. After a few minutes, she emerged from the side entrance, black bike helmet on.

"Enalyn," Andy said. "I think I changed my mind. Tell me about this plan of yours."

17 THE VIDEO

Andy logged into his reactivated YouTube account and found the unpublished video, which he'd called "TIGER SHARK 2 — ANOTHER CRAZY STUNT FROM ANDY KOVACS!"

He added some search terms to the post. He cringed when he entered "Miriam Said," "swimming" and "prank" to the search-term bar.

He hit the play icon. There he was on the screen, wearing a track jacket and swim shorts. He was standing next to a pool. The light shimmering off the water cast a blue-green glow on his face. From the windows in the background, it was clear that it was dark outside.

"Hi, my name is Andy," he watched himself say. "Of course, a lot of you know that. Yes, I am the guy from that Miriam Said video. And that flutterboard surfing video, too. Well, I wanted to do something even more crazy this time!"

On screen, Andy unzipped his track jacket.

"And what embarrassing thing will I do next? I

am going to do something that's a lot tougher than winning a race or surfing on a board. I am going to talk about me.

"You see this pool? It's Earnscliffe Pool, in Brampton, Ontario, Canada. I grew up just a couple of blocks from here, in a townhouse. I went to Cardinal Newman School just down the street. I now go to St. Thomas Aquinas High School.

"My parents put me in swimming lessons when I was little. And within a year, I was taking advanced lessons with kids way older than me. I knew then, well, that in the pool was where I was meant to be. Some people still call me Tiger Shark. It's a cheesy nickname, I know."

The onscreen Andy began to rotate each of his arms.

"Excuse me, I am going to warm up while I talk. Where was I? Oh. Tiger Shark. Well, a long time has gone by. I'm in high school, and swimming is what I love best. I'm in control. No one to depend on. Just me in the water, trying to go as fast as I can. I dreamed that one day I might be in the Olympics.

"And then, as you already know, I did something really stupid. I pranked Miriam Said. You all saw it. And it wasn't funny at all. I found out that it isn't all about me. I wasn't in control. And I don't have any excuses.

"So I wanted to say to Ms. Miriam Said, I am sorry. I really am.

"Because you all saw it, you all think I am, like,

the WORST person in the world. I couldn't go to nationals. I got kicked off the local swim team. I lost my job at the comic shop. And I couldn't even turn on my phone without seeing hundreds, no, thousands of messages from people who want to remind me over and over what a stupid thing I did."

Onscreen Andy crouched down, and most of his body disappeared from the frame. When he rose, he was pulling a set of goggles over his eyes.

"So," Andy said. "Now I am, like, totally humiliated, and maybe I deserve that. But what's worse is that the only time I can do what I love to do is at night, right before the rec centre closes. I can come here and swim. Alone. Not to race. Just to get away from it all. I just wanted to show you who I am. I'm not the guy who went nuts during that interview on the pool deck. This is me."

The camera followed Andy as he walked toward a block at one end of the pool. He got up onto it, and then dropped into the water. The camera then focused near the middle of the pool, where Andy surfaced, arms reaching forward. Andy sped forward in the water, arms pushing through the water. His feet kicked rhythmically. He disappeared again and then flipped as he got close to the wall. His feet sprung off the wall and he was headed the other way, toward the camera.

"Pretty quick," came the voice from the person holding the camera. "Everyone, I'm Andy's friend,

Enalyn. I just wanted to say that I've known Andy for a long time. He's not that jerk you all saw from that Miriam Said video. He can be a real pain sometimes, sure. And he's as clueless as the next guy. But the reaction to what he did, it's out of control. He's down, and everyone out there just keeps kicking him."

Andy pulled himself out of the pool. He sat down on the deck, knees drawn toward his head.

"This is what I do. This is me. And I am sorry."

The video came to an end.

Andy hesitated. The icon was hovering over the PUBLISH button. He clicked his mouse. It was done.

★★★

"So, Andy, are you going to check the comments or not?"

His phone sat on the table. Its screen was dark. Enalyn picked it up and handed it to Andy.

"I mean it. Turn it on," she said, waggling the phone in Andy's face. "I had a peek at some of the comments before I came over. It's not bad."

Andy groaned and took the phone from Enalyn. He pressed the power button in the top corner. After the home screen appeared, he hit the YouTube icon.

The video was already at 775,000 views.

Andy scrolled down the comments section.

Abel12

You think this makes us feel sorry for you? Idiot.

ZaxMcDonald

Well, at least you said you were sorry. That's a start. But get used to swimming alone.

A Real Man

Don't listen to them, Tiger Shark! You don't need to apologize! You put these hijab wearers and feminazis in their place! YEAH!

Shelly Horford

It's people like A Real Man that make me want the world to end. And you too "Tiger Shark." And that girl with the voice in the video . . . WHAT'S WRONG WITH YOU?

Shark Bait

He said he was sorry. I'm so sick of this story. Let's move on.

Zach Attack

You all don't know this guy. I do. I'm on his swim team. He's not a bad guy at all. There's lots of pressure to pull jokes and pranks. I'm sure he was put up to it. Why don't you all lay off?

Zealous
@Zach, how much did "Tiger Shark" pay you to post that CRAP?

Andy stopped scrolling.

"Wait, Zach defended me?" he said. "After what we did to him when he joined the team?"

"Surprised, huh?" said Enalyn. "Zach loves swimming, and knows you're good at it. You're going to have to face it, Andy. Ninety-nine per cent of the people who play sports do it because they like it, not because they want to compete or become pros or go to the Olympics."

Andy put down the phone. There were hundreds more comments on the video's homepage, but he didn't want to look at any more of them.

"Well, other than Zach defending me, I didn't see much good in the comments."

Enalyn grabbed the phone. "Andy, you've got it wrong. I checked something else before I left. Did you know 'Tiger Shark' is trending on Twitter?"

"What?"

Enalyn opened the Twitter app. She entered a search for Tiger Shark.

"There's a series of tweets that are really important, Andy."

She handed the phone back to Andy.

18 THE PRICE

@TheREALMiriamSaid
I saw the new Tiger Shark video. Link here: https://youtube/zznAreema65bl

@TheREALMiriamSaid
I accept the apology. Tiger Shark was kicked out of nationals. Lost his job.

@TheREALMiriamSaid
He's been punished. He's expressed remorse. Check my site for full statement: miriamsaid.blogspot.ca/08/13/Time_To_Forgive

Andy clicked on the link.

> **MiriamSaid.blogspot.ca**
> **TIME TO FORGIVE**
> When my family came to Canada from Egypt, swimming was my one escape. I did not speak English.

I spoke maybe a few words of French. But when I was in the water, I didn't feel like a stranger.

I love this sport. And you know what? I am not the only one. Chances are you may have seen the new video from Andy Kovacs, the young Ontario swimmer who goes by the Tiger Shark nickname.

If you haven't, the link is here: https://youtube/zznAreema65bl

Many of you remember that earlier this summer, Andy hugged me and kissed me on the cheek. As many of you know, my faith requires me to be as modest as possible — and that can be difficult when swim meets require me to be so, well, public.

But what many of you have ignored is that he was punished. Swim Canada didn't give him the chance to go to nationals. And if you'd seen his times at provincials, he had a good shot at winning.

When he got home, he lost his job. And we've just kept talking and talking about him on social media. I tried looking for him, but I'm pretty sure he deleted most of his accounts.

As a whole, we did a good job at making sure that, at every turn, there was another punishment.

At first, I have to admit, I thought, "Good, he deserves it." But then I spoke to my mother and father, and they said that they left a country where you could be jailed for saying the wrong thing about the government. Egypt was a place where the punishments were more severe than the crimes. And they said, "How much is enough?"

I thought about it. How much is enough?

My father told me to always remember that justice and revenge are two separate things. But often we make the mistake of thinking justice and revenge are the same thing — that it's justice if we keep piling on. There is a passage in the Quran: "If you judge, then judge between them with justice (or fairness). Indeed, Allah loves the ones who are just."

Andy Kovacs has lost his shot to win at nationals. His name is all over the Internet. It's time to say, enough. I saw his apology video, and I thought it was brave. We have judged him, but I fear we may have not been just.

Enough.

COMMENTS

Ellie from Edmonton

Miriam, I've dealt with idiots like this throughout my life. I find it hard to forgive them.

Jesse Janes
If that's what you say, Miriam, I respect it.

Quinn17
I have to say that I made about 5–6 posts on Tiger Shark's FB account before he closed it. I think I said some bad things.

Lane Swimmer
I can forgive, I won't forget.

Gator_13
Is there a way that Tiger Shark can go on probation? Let him swim, but if he screws up again, he's gone for good?

Andy thought, I wouldn't screw up again. No more pranks.

"Andy?" Enalyn said. "One more thing. I have a message for you. Coach Ocampo wants you to see him. He'll be at the pool this evening."

★★★

Andy knocked at Coach Ocampo's door.

"Come in."

Andy opened the door and walked into the small office.

"You wanted to see me, Coach?"

"Yes. I'm going to make this short. I saw what you and Enalyn did with the video. It's a start. But don't think I called you here to reinstate you today just because Miriam Said publicly forgave you. That would be wrong."

Andy felt his heart sink. He had hoped that the meeting would go better than this.

"But, and this is a big *but*, I got phone calls from two people today. Travis Holloway and Miriam Said. I asked them what they thought I should do with you. Let it be said that Miss Said thought I should let you swim with COBRA again as soon as possible. If you ever see her at a meet or an event, I suggest you make sure to thank her. Just don't touch her! But Mr. Holloway and I were more of the opinion that we can't simply reinstate you because of a video and the Miriam Said blog post."

"So, what then, Coach?" asked Andy. "I'll do whatever. I'll work with the junior swimmers. I'll reel in the lane ropes after practice . . ."

"Oh I am sure we will have you do those things, when you get back," said the coach. "I've decided that, rather than ban you, you will serve a six-month suspension. The weeks you've already served will go toward those six months. That means you can rejoin the team in January of next year."

"Okay," Andy said.

"I've also spoken to your parents, Andy," said the

coach. "During the six-month suspension, you have one job. School. Next semester, you are to get at least a mark of 75 in your math class. Preferably higher. You must have a total average in all school courses of at least 70, preferably higher. If these conditions aren't met, the suspension stays in place."

Andy nodded.

"Now, Andy, when this is all said and done, you'll have just a few months to get in shape and post great times so you can go to next year's long-course championship. If you do post a qualifying time, Mr. Holloway said he will try to convince Swim Canada to let you swim on a probationary basis. Basically, if you make it to nationals and even button up a shirt wrong, they can send you home."

"Thanks," Andy bleated.

"Andy, this will be tough. The public will be tougher. There will always be people out there who think you should have been banned for life."

"Coach, well, I've started a new Facebook account. I still get hate mail. But it gets less and less every day. Today it was less than fifty. Which is pretty good."

"Andy, I want to remind you, just because you're suspended from COBRA doesn't mean you can't work out on your own. But schoolwork first. Now go. I'll see you in January."

Andy walked out the doors of the Earnscliffe Recreation Centre. The moon hung bright in the sky.

He pulled out his phone from his pocket. He logged in to Twitter so he could reactivate his account. He'd done it just in time: one more day and the account would have been gone forever.

There were thousands of notifications. Andy ignored them all. He had one tweet to make.

@TheREALMiriamSaid Thank you. I won't let you down. Show the world that you're the best.

Andy kept his Twitter app open. It buzzed and buzzed and buzzed as the retweets came.

EPILOGUE

Andy took the bag filled with comics off the counter.

"Um, Andy, you're forgetting something, right?" said Mr. Patel. "Your change."

Mr. Patel handed Andy a couple of loonies and a receipt. "Thanks for shopping at Comic Relief," he said.

"Thanks for letting me back in," said Andy. The first issue of the new *Galaxy Queen vs. Earth's Heroes* crossover series was out.

"Andy, you know, maybe in a bit, you might want to apply to work here again," said Mr. Patel.

"Not right now, thanks," said Andy. "Maybe in a few months. But for now, I really need to focus on my schoolwork."

Andy walked out of the store, went down the escalator and out of the Bramalea City Centre. A cold wind howled through the parkade. There was slush on the ground that got into his socks and boots.

He dashed through the parking lot to the bus terminal. He saw that the 16 Southgate was waiting.

He got through the bus doors just before it was ready to pull out. He flashed his pass and sat down, his bag slung over his shoulder.

When the bus got to Eastbourne Drive, Andy pulled the cord. It stopped just a few metres from the Earnscliffe Recreation Centre.

Andy took a deep breath of cold air and then walked from the bus stop to the rec centre. He went right into the dressing room.

Zach was the first to speak. "Welcome back, Andy."

"Thanks," Andy said softly as he sat down.

"Andy, I want to tell you something."

"What's that, Zach?"

"I've gotten a lot quicker since you last saw me swim. And you're probably a bit out of practice."

"Oh?"

"What I'm saying is that I might need to time *you* with a calendar."

There were a few giggles in the room.

"He's right, you know," said the Eel. "Zach's times have been coming down. He might post a qualifying time for provincials."

Andy nodded. "Well, if a couple more of you slowpokes pick up the pace, we might just be able to put together a relay team for the next big meet."

Andy finished changing and walked out onto the deck. Coach Ocampo was staring out at the pool.

"So, Andy, you ready for this?" said the coach.

"Oh yeah."

"Before you get in the pool, I'll introduce you to one of our new swimmers," said the coach. "I see she just walked onto the deck."

Andy turned around. It was Enalyn, wearing a COBRA swim cap.

"Enalyn?" Andy barked. "You never told me you were coming back!"

"Look, the way I see it, someone has to make sure your pool entries aren't total crap," she said. "But seriously, I missed it. I'm just gonna enjoy myself, try to get better. And of course, I know a certain someone isn't going to be judging me anymore."

Andy shrugged.

"Oh, and I got a few e-mails from Miriam Said, too," said Enalyn. "She ended up being great to chat with. Funny how someone gave her my e-mail address . . ."

Andy smiled. "Well, after the public apology, I e-mailed her a personal one. And she replied. So I told her about you."

"Okay, okay." Coach Ocampo blew on his whistle. "Enough chit-chat. Let's see what you can do, Andy."

Andy windmilled his arms. He did some knee bends. He plunged into the water and did a nice, easy lap. He'd been swimming alone at night so often, he'd forgotten what it was like to have the team there. To have his coach watching to help him improve.

One. Two. Three. Breathe.

GLOSSARY

Swimming is a sport that has its own special language.

BACKSTROKE: A stroke that has the swimmer flat on his or her back, arms reaching back and legs stretched out.

BREASTSTROKE: A stroke where the swimmer's arms begin together, then separate and scoop the water off to the sides. The legs come together and kick apart, like a frog's legs in the water.

BUTTERFLY: A stroke where the arms extend and powerfully enter the water as the body wriggles forward. Extremely difficult on the upper body and shoulders, often beginners aren't allowed to do it.

DAIRY QUEEN (or DAIRY QUEENED): A play on the letters DQ that appear next to a swimmer's name if he or she has been disqualified from a race. A swimmer can get disqualified for touching the lane rope or leaving the blocks too early.

FLIP TURN: To turn and go back in the other direction, the swimmer flips his or her body just before touching the wall. It is timed so the swimmer will flip in the water and end up touching the wall with his or her feet, and then push off to go back in the direction from which he or she came.

FREESTYLE: A race in which swimmers can use any stroke they choose. Almost all swimmers choose to do front crawl because it's the quickest stroke, which is why freestyle races are sometimes mistaken for ones requiring swimmers to use front crawl.

FRONT CRAWL: Most common stroke in swimming. Swimmers arms rotate and extend forward while laying belly-down on water. Feet are extended and legs kick straight. Watch a high-level front crawl race and be amazed how little water is splashed up by the swimmers' strokes. The key is to be as smooth as possible in the water.

LONG COURSE: An Olympic-size pool is 50 metres long. It is called a long course. A 100-metre race would see swimmers go back and forth once.

MEDLEY: A race that combines multiple stroke techniques. A swimmer will do sections of the race using different strokes.

RELAY: A race that has multiple team members (usually four) each swimming an equal amount of laps in a race. A medley relay will see each of the four swimmers taking a specific stroke (freestyle, backstroke, breaststroke and butterfly).

SHORT COURSE: A short-course pool is 25 metres long. Many recreation centres aren't large enough to accommodate 50-metre pools, so many swimmers will train and race in short-course pools, which means they will need to turn more to complete their race distances.

SUICIDE TURN: A lung-busting turn done that's used when coming to the wall off a backstroke. Your palms need to be deep in the water to prepare for a backward flip under the water. The name comes from the difficulty: you can't really see the wall and need to hold your breath for longer.

ACKNOWLEDGEMENTS

I'd like to thank Callum Ng, a senior writer and producer at Olympic.ca and two-time Canadian Interuniversity Sport Swimmer of the Year, for his assistance and advice. I'd also like to acknowledge the aid of Ben Stevenson, manager of production at the Canadian Olympic Committee.

MORE SPORTS, MORE ACTION

www.lorimer.ca/sportsstories

CHECK OUT THESE OTHER SWIMMING STORIES FROM LORIMER'S SPORTS STORIES SERIES:

BREATHING NOT REQUIRED

by Michele Martin Bossley

When eleven-year-old Gracie joins the synchronized swim team, she learns she would do almost anything to be chosen for a solo. Gracie's friend, Laura, loves synchro, too, but she's not going to kill herself over it. Getting ready for the synchronized swimming meet proves a real challenge for the girls and their teammates — in more ways than one.

"A fun, fact-filled novel of synchronized swimming, friendship, jealousy, and family relations... A good sports novel for girls."

— CM Magazine

POOL PRINCESS

by Michele Martin Bossley

Gracie never wanted to move to Calgary. Now she has to make new friends and adjust to a new school. The only bright spot is the synchronized swimming team. Gracie is excited about the chance to perform with some of the best swimmers in Alberta. But not everyone on the team is equally excited about her. After only one practice, one of the swimmers tells Gracie to shape up quickly — or else get out.

Short-listed — Golden Eagle Children's Choice Book Award 2003

TAKING A DIVE

by Michele Martin Bossley

Josie is afraid that her record-breaking swim in the 200-metre butterfly at the Alberta provincial championship was a fluke. As her Calgary swim team trains for a big meet she can't come anywhere near her best time, and sees her dreams of national and Olympic glory slipping away. When she participates in her school's Athletic Challenge, however, she's forced to learn the meaning of "personal best" all over again. The insight she gains there spurs her on when she hits the water again.

Winner — Canadian Children's Book Centre Our Choice Selection 1997

WATER FIGHT!

by Michele Martin Bossley

Josie's sister Melissa is too perfect, better than her in everything — except in the pool. Josie dreams of Olympic swimming gold, and works hard with her Calgary swim team to achieve it. So when Melissa decides to join the team too, Josie is outraged and afraid that, once again, her sister will beat her. But as the big invitational swim meet approaches Melissa acts to help make Josie's dream come true, and forces them both to reconsider the value of sisterhood.

FALSE START

by Sandra Diersch

Caitlynn is no fan of the water, but after breaking her ankle playing soccer, swimming is the safest sport for her. She makes a deal with her grandfather to join a swim team if he'll stay and watch all of her practices. But after Grandpa has a stroke and can no longer tag along, Caitlynn doesn't want to keep up her end of the deal.

Winner — Canadian Children's Book Centre Our Choice Selection 2006

GREAT LENGTHS

by Sandra Diersch

Troy Aitken has just joined the Vancouver club where Jessie Cameron has been swimming for half her life. At first Jessie and her friends are in awe of Troy, who is one of the best athletes they've ever seen. Then the rumours begin to surface... Are the stories true? Jessie's friends believe them, but Jessie isn't sure. Is it fair to turn against Troy on the basis of gossip alone? In the end, Jessie decides she must uncover the truth for herself.

SWIM TO WIN

by Vallery Hyduk

Birch Hill Swim Club has a new coach and the team's star swimmer, eighth-grader Lasha Boyko, couldn't be more excited. Even though the lanky swimmer comes from an immigrant Ukrainian family of modest means, she dreams big. The coach has a track record of producing Olympians and Lasha wants to be her next star. The hitch is that she's one of the fiercest trainers in world. To achieve her lofty goals, Lasha must look within herself to find the strength. Can she be a champion?

"Along with generous measures of information about competition swimming (delivered in context, not as info dumps), readers will get a solid sense of the inner toughness required to excel... Salutary reading for young athletes with big dreams."

— Booklist Online (US)

SINK OR SWIM

by William Pasnak

Dario Cavalito has his summer plans all mapped out: he's going to split his time between the basketball court and his Uncle Vinny's café. His plans are derailed, however, when his mother tells him he's going away for the summer — to a water sports camp. Dario can barely do the dog paddle, but he finds he actually kind of likes the water. As the camp's sailing regatta approaches, he fights to overcome the last of his reluctance and to win big.

Winner — Canadian Children's Book Centre Our Choice Selection 1995

"Dario's first-person narrative is energetic... Sink or Swim has its fair share of funny gags... sports enthusiasts will certainly enjoy Pasnak's vivid descriptions of the summer world of swimming, volleyball and sailing."

— Kenneth Oppel, Quill & Quire

LORIMER

FLIP TURN

by Monique Polak

Victoria Miller is a hard-working member of a Montreal swim team, who has been training six days a week for four years. That's what it takes to keep up with her teammate and rival, Svetlana. Most of the other swimmers are spurred on by their parents — but not Victoria. In fact, her mother doesn't seem to be interested in much of anything these days, and her father has buried himself in work. When the family situation takes a grim turn, Victoria finds help — in and out of the pool — from the person she least expects.